JAKE ATLAS

AND THE QUEST FOR
THE CRYSTAL MOUNTAIN

JAKE ATLAS

AND THE QUEST FOR THE CRYSTAL MOUNTAIN

ROB LLOYD JONES

WALKER
BOOKS

First published in Great Britain 2019 by Walker Books Ltd
87 Vauxhall Walk, London SE11 5HJ

2 4 6 8 10 9 7 5 3 1

Text © 2019 Rob Lloyd Jones
Cover illustration © 2019 Petur Antonsson

This book has been typeset in ITC Veljovic

Printed and bound by CPI Group (UK) Ltd, Croydon CR0 4YY

British Library Cataloguing in Publication Data:
a catalogue record for this book is available from the British Library

ISBN 978-1-4063-8500-7

www.walker.co.uk

For Nicole, Daniel, Daisy,
Imogen and Zephy –
future treasure hunters, all of them

1

"T-minus four minutes. Pan, are you in position?"

"I'm ready."

"Jane? Are you in position?"

"Yes, John, I am *still* in position."

"Jake? Are you in position?"

"What does T-minus actually mean?"

"Excuse me?"

"You always say T-minus when you do count-downs. What does the T mean? Turtle?"

"I... Why would it mean turtle?"

"Dunno. I'm looking at a statue of a turtle."

"Why are you looking at a statue of a turtle, Jake?"

"There's one over here, on this side of the museum."

"Jake, focus on the mission. The statues!"

"Chill out, Mum."

"Don't you tell me to chill out, young man."

"T-minus three minutes. Is everyone in position?"

"Stop asking that, John! Everyone is in position apart from Jake, who is looking at turtles and not the statues."

"I *am* looking at a statue. A statue of a turtle."

"The *terracotta warriors*, Jake. The mission is the terracotta warriors."

"T-minus two and a half minutes."

"*Time!* T means time, doesn't it?"

"Yes, Jake, T means time. Now, are you ready?"

"Guys, I was *born* ready."

I turned from the statue cabinet to gaze across one of the most famous archaeological sites in the world. Six months ago I'd have been surprised to learn that there were *any* famous archaeological sites in the world, and definitely would not have known what they were. A lot has changed since then. I've gone from being a school dropout and a thief to... Well, actually, I'm still a school dropout and a thief, but it's different now. My parents have *taken* me out of school, to train me to be a treasure hunter.

We'd been travelling the world for half a year, searching for mysterious emerald tablets before a creepy organization – we called them the People of the Snake – could get their hands on them. The tablets led to the Hall of Records, a secret store of knowledge about a lost civilization. That sounded cool, but this bit wasn't: whatever had wiped the civilization out might come again, and the People of the Snake were trying to hide it from the world. Their leader, the Snake Lady (her real name was Marjorie), *wanted* to let the catastrophe happen, in order to reduce the world's population and manage it – she wanted to decide who lived and who died.

That wasn't happening as long as we could stop it. That's why we were in China, at the Museum of the Terracotta Army.

A huge concrete hangar covered eight long trenches filled with life-sized statues of ancient Chinese soldiers made from terracotta clay. I mean *filled* – there were around eight thousand statues in the trenches, buried over two thousand years ago to guard a nearby tomb of an emperor.

A tomb that we were about to rob.

The museum was packed with tourists, who could only view the fragile statues from raised platforms. They pushed and shoved while tour guides shouted and guards barked at anyone who leaned over the railings to snap a selfie. It was all pretty stressful, but that was perfect. We needed to cause chaos, and chaos works better with lots of people.

Some files we'd swiped from the Snake Lady said that one of the emerald tablets was in the emperor's tomb. In a document by a craftsman who built the tomb, we'd learned of a secret hidden in one of these terracotta warriors – a clue to a safe passage inside. He'd even left a map leading to the statue.

We'd planned this part of the mission from our hideout in Beijing. Pan was outside keeping watch for our enemies, while my parents were on a platform on the other side of the museum in case any of those enemies stormed through the entrance. We spoke to one another through microphones in our smart-goggles – super-high-tech pieces of kit that looked like wraparound sunglasses.

"T-minus one minute," Dad said.

"I have the target," Mum replied. "The middle trench, thirty-seventh statue in the line. John, can you confirm?"

Dad scanned the trenches until he found the statue. "Confirmed. That's the statue we need. T-minus twenty seconds."

"All right," Mum agreed. "I'm going over."

"What?" I hissed. "*I* go over. That's the plan. You and Dad stay up top to deal with the guards."

"It's too risky, Jake."

"So you want *me* to fight the guards?"

Mum swore under her breath. She knew I was right.

"T-minus five seconds."

"Stop saying that, John!"

"Two seconds..."

A cry rang out across the heads of the terracotta warriors, and then another, as clouds of grey smoke engulfed the tourists. The smoke was harmless – pumping from canisters we'd hidden around the platforms – but no one else knew that, so in seconds people were screaming and running for the exits.

"Jake, get ready," Dad warned. "Any second now..."

Someone jumped over the railings to where the statues stood. Now another tourist leaped too, dropping ten feet to the trenches and calling for her husband to lower their children.

"Jake, now!" Dad urged.

I grabbed the railing and jumped. A tourist caught me, which was nice, and then screamed, *"We're all going to die!"* in my face, which really wasn't. I shoved him away, waving my arms to clear the smoke that had drifted down to the trenches.

"OK, guide me to it!" I called.

Dad had "geo-locked" the statue we were after, so it showed up as a glowing orange blob on his smartgoggles, while my own heat signature appeared in green.

"Get across the first trench," he instructed through his goggles' microphone.

"Jake," Mum warned, "do not damage any of the statues."

"I know, Mum..."

It would have been quicker if I hadn't had to be so careful. The terracotta warriors were packed into the trench with barely a foot between them, so it took ages to squeeze through to a ladder on the other side. I scrambled up and ran along the ledge between the trenches.

"Keep going," Dad said.

"Uh, guys?" My sister, who was still outside the

museum, sounded worried. "The People of the Snake's goons are on their way. About a dozen of them."

"Only a dozen?" Dad said. "OK, let them come."

If my dad sounded relaxed it was because we'd met these mercenaries before; they were ex-soldiers who helped the People of the Snake guard their secrets. They were thugs, and no match for trained treasure hunters like my parents.

"Jake," Dad called through his goggles, "you're almost at the statue."

The mercenaries, dressed in black like Special Forces soldiers, stormed through the museum entrance and onto the platform where my parents were positioned. Each of them carried an electro-laser gun with a crab-claw barrel that fired bolts of lightning powerful enough to drop an elephant. They didn't get a chance to use them. Mum and Dad were on them in seconds. Dad swung punches like a heavyweight boxer. Mum was like an acrobat, all flips, ducks and spinning kicks. I was about to go back to help, but Mum barked at me between punches.

"Don't worry about us, Jake! Just get to that statue. It's right below you now, at the edge of the trench."

I slid into the pit, careful to avoid bumping into any of the tightly packed statues. Knocking one over would send the others tumbling like dominoes. I shifted around and then flinched in fright as I came face to face with one of them. It was so lifelike that I half-expected it to reach out and grab me. This was where I would find a clue that would guide us into the emperor's tomb – but where was it?

"Jake, hurry up," Dad grunted. "The smoke is clearing; you'll be seen."

"Torch," I said.

A beam shone from the frame of my smart-goggles. I ran it around details carved in clay: the statue's chain-mail skirt and tunic, its goatee beard and its fierce, glaring eyes. And then...

I crouched and aimed the light at the statue's heel. There, carved from jade, was something that looked like a key. I pulled it out and shoved it in my pocket.

"Got it!" I announced.

"Get to the exit," Mum instructed. She paused to execute a flying roundhouse kick to one of the goons. "We're right behind you."

Considering the circumstances – alarms ringing, mercenaries attacking my parents, and me trapped in the middle – it seemed strange that everything was going to plan.

The smoke was beginning to clear. If I could get back to the platform, I should be able to reach the exit and—

THUD.

A steel barrier slid down over the exit. The impact rattled the platforms and caused the terracotta warriors to shudder.

From outside the museum Pan asked, "What was that?"

"The way out," I gasped. "It's not a way out any more."

Mum cursed. "Pandora, are there any other exits?"

"Only one," she replied. "An archaeologists' store-room at the far end of Jake's trench. It connects to the museum's cooling system. But I don't know how you'd make it there."

"Jake?" Dad said. "We need a plan!"

This next bit is going to sound strange. As well as being awesome treasure hunters, my parents are college professors: brain-box experts in ancient history, archaeology and ancient languages. My twin sister, Pan, is even smarter. She's a genius, with a photographic memory, who can learn stuff crazy fast. I guess she stole my "clever gene" at birth, because I'd always struggled in school or when we were planning a mission. But when it came to planning *during* a mission, they all looked to me. I had this weird skill to be able to think under pressure and find ways out of danger. It had saved our lives a few times recently, and I needed it now more than ever.

I breathed in, held my breath, and let it go slowly – a calming technique Mum had taught me to help me focus. I felt as if someone had hacked into my head, someone much cleverer than me. My eyes darted, studying my surroundings. Plans of escape flashed through my mind. I discarded one, then another, until I was left with a single possibility.

"Pan," I said. "Can you open the door to the cooling

system from the outside with your skeleton key?"

"I... Yes, but Jake you can't reach that door without being shot by the mercenaries."

"Don't worry, just open it."

The smoke had almost faded and the mercenaries would see me soon. They'd have no hesitation about firing into these statues. To reach that door I needed a new smokescreen.

"Jake?" Mum said. "What are you doing?"

"Don't worry, I've got a plan. Pan and I can still get to the tomb and find the emerald tablet."

"Jake," Mum pleaded, "please don't do what I think you're about to do."

I didn't *want* to do it, but I had to reach the door. If I didn't make it, everything we'd accomplished during the last six months would be for nothing.

"Jake," Mum warned. "Don't do it!"

"I'm sorry," I croaked. "I'm sorry, I'm sorry..."

I reached out to the nearest statue and pushed. Remember what I said about dominoes?

The clay soldier fell back and crashed into the one behind it, which tumbled into the next one, which hit another. Each warrior shattered as it fell, causing clouds of red clay dust to fill the trench like a sandstorm on Mars.

Or a smokescreen.

"Jake!" Dad barked. "Go!"

I charged though the thickening cloud. My boots crunched over clay rubble as more statues toppled in my path. I spat dust and rubbed it from my goggles, so I could just about see the service door.

"Pan," I wheezed. "Have you got that door open yet?"

"I'm on the other side," she said. "But I can't unlock it..."

A livid blue blast of energy hit the trench wall as one of the mercenaries opened fire into the dust cloud. Splinters of rock sprayed my face. I staggered away from the door as more stun blasts fired from the platform. I'd got lucky so far, but one of those shots would hit me soon...

Think, Jake, think!

"Mum," I called. "Would a blast from a stun gun break that door open?"

"One blast? No."

"How about a dozen?"

"Yes."

"Pan, get back from the door," I yelled. "Get far back!"

I leaped up, waving my arms and calling to the mercenaries. "Hey! Down here, you dimwits!"

A lightning storm of stun blasts struck the rubble and the trench walls. At least a dozen of the shots hit the metal door, which crumpled like paper and flew off its hinges. Screaming all the way, I charged and leaped through the empty doorway.

A hand yanked me up and instinctively I lashed out, shoving someone back.

"Hey!" a voice snapped. "It's me!"

It was Pan. Her face looked ghostly pale against her raven-black dyed hair, and her eyes were wide and wild beneath her smart-goggles, but she mustered a grin.

"Come on!" she urged.

I followed her along a passage lined with cooling ducts, and up an iron spiral of stairs. At the top, Pan shoved open a door she'd left unlocked, and we stumbled out into dazzling daylight.

"Are you OK?" she asked.

"I ... I think so."

"Good, because we're only halfway though this. Come on!"

Look, I know all that sounds crazy. But, really, it wasn't too unusual a morning for my family. What was about to happen, though, was different. No matter how clever my parents or sister were, or how quickly I can think when in danger, none of us could have stopped it from coming, or from changing our lives for ever. If we'd known, we would have run as fast as we could in the opposite direction, far away from the emperor's tomb...

2

The area outside the museum was in chaos. Everyone was running and screaming, scrambling and shoving, fighting to get back onto coaches. Someone tumbled into a stall selling replica terracotta warriors, sending them scattering.

My sister pulled me along as we sprinted past a golden statue of a Chinese emperor pointing in the direction of his tomb a kilometre away. We'd trained at running the distance, but had never covered it as fast as we did then, fuelled by fear and adrenaline.

"There!" Pan cried. "The tomb!"

We'd seen some incredible things over the past six months – stunning Egyptian temples and intricately carved Aztec shrines – but this was not like them. The tomb was the height of an ancient pyramid and about the same shape, but it looked like a plain old hill.

The tomb belonged to Emperor Qui Shin Huangdi,

who had united China two thousand years ago. He'd covered the hill in rocks and trees to make it look normal and hide it from robbers. There were thought to be traps inside too, crossbows rigged to fire and poisonous streams of mercury. No one had dared go in – until now.

I touched my pocket as I ran, making sure I still had the jade key. I guessed we had to find some sort of secret door, so it was good that we had the place to ourselves.

Only...

I stopped and looked back along the path. Something wasn't right. It was just a feeling, an instinct I'd learned to trust...

Pan glared at me, wiping hair from her eyes. "What's wrong?"

"Why isn't anyone coming after us?" I asked.

"That's good, right?"

I wasn't so sure. "The People of the Snake know what we're after. They should have mercenaries guarding the tomb. We'd planned for that, remember?"

"What are you saying?"

I didn't know. "They knew we'd run for this hill if we got the key," I said.

I turned again, staring at the blue sky beyond the tomb. A strange noise began to echo, like a steam train at half speed. *Choka choka choka choka...*

"Jake, what is that?"

As the noise grew louder, my heart seemed to stop

and then start again at triple speed. I knew that the Snake Lady would do *anything* to stop us from getting that emerald tablet.

I grabbed Pan's arm. "Run!"

Now we were sprinting again, this time away from the tomb.

Choka, choka, choka, choka...

I snatched a look back and saw a dark shape rise over the hill like a sea monster surfacing from the deep. It blocked the sun, swallowing us with its shadow: the unmistakable silhouette of a helicopter.

"Jake! Get down!"

Pan dragged me to the ground as something fired. I glimpsed a rush of flame. The missile slammed into the side of the hill, followed by a second of silence.

And then the hill exploded.

It seemed to burst from within. Earth, rocks and shattered tree trunks fired in every direction. We were hit by a wall of mud, and then a blast wave sent us tumbling into a tree. Gold and silver treasures thumped down around us.

And then it was over.

The only sound was our frantic breathing, and the *choka, choka, choka* growing distant as the helicopter flew away. Pan and I stayed huddled together, shaking from shock and spitting out mud.

"Are you alive?" I grunted.

"I ... I'm not sure. Are you?"

The blast had knocked the wind out of me, but

I wasn't really hurt. My sister helped me up and we leaned against each other, staring at the destruction. The centre of the hill had been blown away, as if someone had grabbed at a cake with their fist. Most of the tomb lay scattered around us: collapsed walls, broken statues, metal objects jutting out at odd angles. Beyond, the silhouette of the helicopter grew smaller as it flew into the sun.

"Pandora! Jake!"

Our parents raced along the path, their expressions torn between horror at what they were seeing and relief that we were alive. They grabbed us, hugged us, checked us for injuries, and then swapped us over and hugged and checked again.

At first we let them, too shaken to do much else. But as Dad inspected me again, I spotted something amidst the wreckage. I pulled away and staggered to one of the few surviving trees.

"There..." I gasped. "It's there!"

Stuck in the lower branches was the emerald tablet. It may have been thousands of years old and splattered with mud, but as I pulled it out it gleamed like a freshly cut gemstone. It was just like the others we'd found, covered in script and symbols, and with a carving of a coiled snake eating its own tail. We had thought that was the symbol of the lost civilization, but it was also the emblem of the People of the Snake. The Snake Lady wore it proudly as a brooch. Well, get a load of this, Marjorie!

I raised the tablet triumphantly, grinning at my family.

"We did it," I croaked.

None of them smiled back. They just stared at the destruction; one of the world's greatest archaeological sites was now in ruins.

"*What* did we do?" Mum asked.

3

It was a ten-hour train ride to Beijing. We had a cabin to ourselves, double bunk beds separated by a tiny gap. Pan fell asleep with her hood pulled over her head and guitars blaring from her headphones. She often listened to heavy metal music to get to sleep, which is weird when you think about it, but it's best not to think about my sister too much or *everything* seems weird.

Dad nodded off too, snoring like a hippo, feet hanging over the edge of his bunk. I didn't understand how they *could* sleep. I was buzzing like I'd been plugged into a power socket. We had the third tablet! I lay with it clutched to my chest – a laptop-sized emerald slab, carved with ancient script and symbols that we hadn't been able to decipher. We'd needed one more tablet to crack the code, and this was it. I couldn't wait to get back to our hideout in Beijing. We'd hoped the tablets would lead us to the lost civilization's Hall of Records, and now we were about to find out if they did.

Mum didn't look so happy about it all. She sat staring at her reflection in the window and stroking her necklace pendant, an amulet of the Ancient Egyptian mother goddess, Isis. It was an artefact she'd stolen on one of her first missions with Dad, over thirty years ago.

My parents used to be normal archaeologists. But after they learned how many relics were being sold on the black market, they decided to get to them first and make sure they ended up in museums. They'd travelled the world, trained in fighting and technology, and they were *good*. Go into any major museum and you'll see at least a dozen things my parents rescued, although I promised I'd never say which.

When Mum got pregnant they settled down as college professors. But after they learned about the People of the Snake and their plan to let millions of people die, Mum and Dad went to Egypt to stop them. That's where me and Pan discovered their secret. Since then they'd been training us to become treasure hunters too.

The training was hard, and it had taken ages for Mum and Dad to trust us. But now we were close to working out where the tablets led. So I didn't understand why Mum looked so grumpy.

Outside, the sun was setting, slashing the sky pink as I stared out at the countryside – a muddy river, hazy terraced hillsides, power lines and power stations. I did actually fall asleep. I guess I was too tired not to. When I woke, the train had stopped and the tablet was no longer in my hands.

I shifted up, rubbing my eyes. Pan was in her bunk, guitar music still blaring from under her hood, and Dad was snoring louder than ever.

Mum was gone.

Maybe she needed the loo? But why had she taken the tablet?

I felt it again. A tingle, an instinct. Something was wrong.

I opened the cabin door and stepped into the train corridor, blinking in the glare of its flickering strip light. Rubbing mist from a window, I could just pick out some details in the dark. We had stopped at a station in the middle of nowhere, with a single platform and a few rusty cargo trains. The door at the end of the corridor was open, and the train guards outside were squabbling. Beyond them, something darted between the trains.

"Mum?" I breathed.

I waited until the guards weren't looking, and jumped out. The cold chased away the last of my sleep. I wished I'd put on my coat. Stars shivered in the coal-black sky, but I couldn't see the moon.

Double-checking that no one was watching, I ran across the tracks to where I'd seen Mum disappear between the trains. Beyond was rough countryside, and I could just see her trail through the long grass.

I followed her to the edge of a small lake. She stood staring across the starlit water, the emerald tablet in her hand. She seemed to be in a trance, like a sleepwalker. I was about to call to her, when she stepped back and raised the tablet as if to throw it into the water!

"Mum!" I shouted.

She whirled around, suddenly alert.

"Stay right there!" she snapped.

Icy wind swept from the lake, but a fire was rising in my belly. What was Mum thinking?

"Go back, Jake."

"Not without that tablet," I replied.

"You don't understand. This tablet is a curse. They all are."

"A curse? What do you mean?"

"We've searched the world for these, Jake, and where have they led? On a path of destruction."

"That's not true."

"You destroyed the *Terracotta Army*, Jake."

I had known this was going to come up, but I hadn't expected it to be so soon. If there had been any other way to get that tablet I'd have taken it. But what we were trying to do was too important to fail. The end justified the means, even if the means were pretty crazy.

"If I hadn't done that we'd have been caught," I said. "We'd be in a Chinese prison right now."

The tablet trembled in her hands. "But the Terracotta Army would still be in one piece. And the emperor's tomb."

"That doesn't matter," I shot back. "Not compared to our mission. We'll be able to decipher them now, to find out where they lead."

"Jake, have you ever considered that maybe they lead nowhere?"

"That's not true," I insisted. "The Snake Lady wouldn't be going to so much trouble if it was. She just blew up a tomb to protect that secret."

"Stop reminding me!"

"But, Mum—"

"The Terracotta Army, Jake! The emperor's tomb! The tomb beneath the Great Pyramid, the Temple of Isis, the Aztec tombs in Honduras. They're all gone."

She raised the tablet again.

"No, don't!" I cried. "If we don't follow where that tablet leads, then all that destruction will have been for nothing. And then Marjorie will win. Something wiped out that lost civilization and it might come back. The People of the Snake will keep that secret, Mum, if we don't get find the Hall of Records first. You *know* they will."

She sighed, but lowered the tablet. Ultimately, that artefact was one of the things she had sworn to protect. And also, she was a treasure hunter and this was the greatest treasure hunt in history. She couldn't walk away from it.

Behind us, the train driver blew the whistle, urging anyone who had left to hurry back. Mum walked past me and placed the tablet by my feet.

"Take it," she said. "I don't want to see it for a while."

I snatched it up a little too eagerly. "Don't worry, Mum," I called. "We're doing the right thing."

"Are we, Jake?" she replied.

4

We'd been planning the mission at the emperor's tomb for two months and we needed a break, but we weren't about to get one. Now that we had the third tablet, we could finally decipher the artefacts' signs and symbols – and discover where they led.

We'd been hiding out in Beijing, which is a bonkers place. There should be another word to describe Beijing, something more than just city. It's a *super* city. It makes London look like a village.

The streets were crammed with more cars than I thought could exist, and people wore masks over their faces so they didn't breathe the fumes that hung in a grey veil.

But I loved Beijing. We'd rented a house in an old part of town, among a tangle of lanes called *hutongs*, full of steamy dumpling shacks, stalls selling fish, people hanging out washing, kids kicking footballs.

This sprawling maze was a perfect place to disappear.

The hutongs weaved among traditional Chinese homes that were over five hundred years old. You could tell from their curving tiled roofs and brass door knockers that the houses had once been grand, but those days were long gone. Now their interiors were mostly crumbling walls and broken windows, while outside stood greasy extractor fans, generators and air conditioning units belching smoke.

The bungalow we were staying in was derelict, with three rooms surrounding a smashed concrete courtyard. We'd turned one of the rooms into mission HQ. Its walls were covered in satellite photos and blueprints of the Terracotta Warrior Museum. In the middle, a flat glass screen lay on a trestle table – a cool bit of kit called a holosphere.

Mum pressed her thumb against it, and a keyboard appeared on the glass. A second later two holograms beamed from the screen – pin-sharp 3D images of the emerald tablets we'd found so far. We'd left the real ones in a hiding place in London, with instructions for them to be sent to the British Museum if we were caught.

"Here they are," Dad said, in his 'serious scholar' voice. "The tablets from Egypt and Honduras. Each found in a tomb of someone from a much older civilization that was wiped out. Its survivors spread around the world and established new cultures. They were remembered as gods, buried in crystal coffins decorated with the same symbol – a snake eating its own tail. In each coffin was one of these emerald tablets, which we believe lead to a lost store of knowledge detailing the history of this civilization, known as the Hall of Records. We hope to learn where the people were from, what happened to them, and when the destruction will happen again. We've not been able to decipher the script with just two tablets. Now we have a third, and a chance."

"We know all of this," Mum muttered. "Why are you telling us?"

"Just sounded good," Dad replied.

"It sounded silly," Mum said. "Jake, bring the tablet over."

I clutched it tighter to my chest. My dad and sister didn't know that Mum had almost thrown it away last night, and I didn't plan to tell them, but I wasn't sure I trusted her not to try it again. I think she sensed it, because she smiled and held out her hand.

"Let's see what it says, shall we?"

She took the tablet and laid it on the holosphere screen. Lasers rose from the glass and scanned the artefact, changing colour as they mapped its markings. After a few seconds, another hologram beamed up – a perfect image of the third tablet.

Mum slid the actual tablet back to me across the table.

"You *can* chuck that now," she said.

She was joking, but not smiling. Her jaw was locked, her eyes fixed on the holograms.

"John," she ordered, "run cross-checks on word frequency distribution on all three tablets, a full lexical analysis. Pan, check for phonographic graphemes, and watch out for silent determinatives. I'll look for repeating syntax and typographic ligatures. And, Jake?"

She glanced at me. "Make us a cup of tea."

I'd have flipped at her for that once, but I was cool with it now. My strength definitely wasn't lexical analysis, whatever that meant. Even so, I didn't want to make tea. I'd miss this moment, the big unveiling of the script.

"Well?" I asked, impatiently. "What do the tablets say?"

They all looked away from the holograms, and to me.

"You know this is going to take a while, right?" Pan said.

"What, like a few minutes?"

Pan shook her head.

"A few hours?" I asked.

She shook her head again.

"Well, how long, then?"

"A few weeks, Jake."

I stared at her, and then at my mum and dad, who nodded, agreeing with the timeline.

"Really?" I groaned. "I thought you'd press a button and something clever would happen."

Pan turned back to her work, tapping her head. "The clever stuff is happening in *here*, Jake."

Yeah, but slowly. I guessed I'd be making a lot of tea. But we were still ahead of the People of the Snake, so we were in no rush. And we could all use a little time to recover from that last mission.

"Tea, Jake," Mum snapped.

"OK! I need a wee first."

"Don't go far."

I left them fiddling with their holograms and headed out into the hutongs to find a toilet. There were no street lamps, so at night the lanes relied on light from the shops, bare bulbs and flickering neon signs. My stomach grumbled as I passed my favourite food stall, Mi Chi'o Dumplings, and smelled steamed fish and fried meat. Close by, a gang of men squabbled over how to fix a motorbike. A woman painted Chinese letters on a wall, while a really fat man watched from a tiny plastic stool. With each new sight I felt better about how long it would take to crack the code. A couple more weeks hanging around these lanes would suit me fine.

Further along the alley, a woman selling Hello Kitty balloons had fallen asleep on the job. I crept closer and tied the balloons to a drainpipe so they didn't float free. Right then, someone passed behind me – a tourist in a baseball cap. I didn't know why, but something made me notice him. As I watched, the guy stopped to check a guidebook in a shop light, and then touched his ear.

Was he wearing a comms bud?

Maybe it was a headphone or a hearing aid, but I couldn't ignore that tingle in my belly. The man wore sunglasses too, which was strange at night. Unless they were *special* sunglasses...

I followed him back the way I had come. He stopped again outside Mr Chi's Dumplings, and I caught a glimpse of his face. It was all angles and bone structure: a military face. He touched his earpiece again – three quick taps.

My senses were on full alert; I'd even forgotten that I needed a wee.

The man stopped again at a junction between two hutongs, where a couple of boys booted a football off the walls. I ducked into an alley and watched from a distance. Two other figures appeared from the opposite direction – a man and a woman, also in caps. To anyone else they looked like friends meeting up for dinner. To me, they were big trouble.

We'd been found.

My heart was thumping as hard as the football against the walls. I darted down the alley to a climbing frame of rubbish bins and extractor fans, and scrambled up onto the roof of one of the houses. Staying low, I moved along the tiles, spying on the bad guys below. They'd stopped outside one of the houses. The two men guarded its entrance, while the woman went inside.

I crept higher up the roof so I could peer over the

front wall of the house opposite. In one of its rooms I saw my family around the holosphere, studying the hologram tablets.

I remained as still as a gargoyle as the woman gave several hand signals. A dozen more figures appeared from the shadows. They sprang over walls and slid down from the roofs, all armed with crab-claw plasma guns.

Then they launched their attack.

5

I crouched lower on the tiles, watching the Snake Lady's mercenaries storm the house on the other side of the hutong. A door was kicked open, a window smashed, and a dozen of the goons charged into the room where my mum, dad and sister stood around the holosphere. None of my family turned as the thugs opened fire, strobe-lighting the room with energy blasts. The holosphere screen flipped up and smashed against a wall. That many shots would have knocked my actual family out for a week. But, come on, do you really think I'd just sit there and watch that happen?

We had a plan.

We hadn't just rented *one* house, but also the house on the other side of the alley. We'd rigged it with a trilateration scrambler, a gadget that redirects tracking devices to its location. It led the mercenaries there, where they saw holograms of my family hard at work in the house opposite, the one from which I was watching.

I scrambled to the other side of the roof, slid down a drainpipe to the courtyard and charged to the room where my family was *really* working.

"Mercenaries just hit the decoy house," I cried.

My family turned and stared.

"Did you get the tea?" Dad asked.

"What? Are you joking?"

They were, thank God.

"There's no need to panic," Mum assured me. "They have no idea where we are. I'll gather our things. John, set the chargers. Jake, keep watch. We leave in five minutes using the tunnel, as planned."

"Five minutes?" Pan protested. "This decipherment programme needs *days*. We've got nothing from the tablets so far."

"We don't have a choice, Pandora," Mum snapped, shoving our belongings into duffel bags. "We can't be here any longer."

Pan shot me a look for support. "Jake?"

I slid my smart-goggles on and gave them an order. *"Perimeter security cameras."*

The lenses showed a live video of the hutong, which was now filled with mercenaries. It wouldn't be long until they worked out where we really were.

"I'm with Mum on this one," I said.

Pan swore at me and turned back to the holosphere.

Her hands sped around the glass screen, tapping keys and turning hologram dials. The projections spun in the air, separating into sections that rotated in different directions. It was like someone doing three Rubik's Cubes at the same time.

"Wait," she called. "I've got something. A single word repeats on all the tablets."

Dad rushed to see. "What word?"

Pan extracted a section of one of the holograms, a sliver of light. "Here," she breathed. "This is it."

"Run it through a linguistic analysis programme," Dad said.

Mum pulled a rug away from the floor, revealing an iron hatch. She yanked it open and began dropping duffel bags into the underground tunnel.

"John," she called, "set the charges for two minutes. We can't let them get that information."

"I need more time," Pan protested.

"We have to go right now," Mum insisted.

Dad typed into the screen beside Pan and a flashing red dot projected from the glass. He'd set a self-destruct timer to delete the information stored in the holosphere. In two minutes all of our research would be gone. We needed to be too.

"Jake," Mum called. "Where are they?"

My goggles showed eight mercenaries by the entrance. "Right outside," I replied. "They're being cautious, but they know we're here."

"The translation is so close," Pan groaned.

"So are the bad guys, Pan!"

I tried to pull her away, but she shrugged me off. Her eyes glowed with the light from the word she'd extracted from the tablets, which was now a high-speed scroll of characters from ancient languages.

"Look, it's working!"

Even Mum couldn't stop herself from looking as one of the symbols stopped spinning and settled on a single character.

"It looks like a six-letter word," Pan said. "The first is a K."

The red light flashed brighter. "Thirty seconds until charges detonate," Dad warned. "Get away from the screen; the whole thing's going to blow."

"Twenty seconds," Pan hissed. "That's all it needs..."

"The mercenaries are in the courtyard," I gasped.

"Let's go!" Mum demanded.

"Ten seconds..."

"Our time is up, Pandora."

"There! Look!"

The translation was complete. A single word hung in the air, turning and twisting, making it hard to read.

"It says ... *Kailas*," Pan said. "OK, *now* let's go."

We raced to follow Mum and Dad through the hatch, but all their urgency had suddenly vanished. They stood staring at the word spinning above the holosphere, as if a ghost had risen from the screen.

Mum touched the amulet around her neck.

"Kailas," she whispered.

That word meant something to my parents, but there was no time to ask because right then four things happened. The charges detonated in a chaos of electricity, a lightning storm across the holosphere. At the same time one of the windows smashed, an energy pulse grenade flew through the broken glass and ten mercenaries burst into the room.

We didn't see the explosion – by then Dad had slammed the hatch and bolted it from the inside – but we heard it, and felt the tunnel walls tremble, as we fled together through the underground darkness. All of our information had just been destroyed, and all we had to show for it was a single word.

And I *really* needed a wee.

6

"No trace at all?"

The mission report trembled in the mercenary's grip. He scanned it again, as if he might somehow locate the Atlas family among its densely typed notes.

"Unfortunately not, Councillor," he said, in a voice as unsteady as his hands. "They believe the boy alerted his family. Apparently he followed them as they approached the hideout."

"He followed them?"

"Apparently."

Marjorie breathed in deeply, held her breath, and let it go. It was a calming technique she had learned from Jake Atlas, but it didn't work.

"The team that raided the family's headquarters," she said. "They were, I was assured, among the best surveillance squads in any military."

"I..."

"And yet they were undone by a twelve-year-old boy."

"I... He is a very gifted—"

"Very gifted, yes I know. But he hasn't served in the military. He wasn't part of the protection unit for a United States president, or an intelligence officer with Mossad. Or was he, this twelve-year-old boy?"

"No. None of those things, ma'am."

"No. None of those things. Yet still the family escaped."

"The council are gathered, ma'am. They wish to speak with you."

"Of course they do."

The mercenary took this as his cue to scuttle off, whimpering with relief.

Marjorie stepped up to the headquarters' only window, a sliver of bombproof glass with a view across Paris to the Sacré-Cœur, a space rocket-shaped basilica that soared above the patchwork rooftops. The council were waiting. Well, let them wait. Too often they whistled and she came running.

Music began to play in her head, as deep and rich as if she stood beside her record player. It was an aria from Puccini's *La Bohème*, the tragic tale of the Parisian seamstress and her lover. It played in her head almost every day. It haunted her. It was silly to think she could ever know love like that, but she had never known *anything* like that. This job was her whole life.

She looked down, only now realizing that her hand was clasped tightly around her brooch, the emerald symbol of the organization, the sign of a snake eating its own tail. Her work was the most precious thing in her life. She had sacrificed everything to serve the organization, but now the entire operation was on the verge of collapse. It shouldn't have been that hard to locate nine emerald tablets, decipher their codes and discover where they led. The organization had unlimited authority and budget, guaranteed by a classified treaty of thirty-two nations. They had headquarters around the world, mercenaries to guard their secrets, and agreements with a dozen professional treasure hunters. All of the tablets should now be in their possession. They should be well on their way to unlocking their secrets.

But.

But, but, but.

The Atlas family had got involved.

Two treasure hunters past their prime – although still the best in the business – and two children with limited training, yet surprising natural skills. At first they had been a thorn, an annoyance that should have been plucked out. But they had survived ambushes, attacks, a plane crash, a flood. An entire mountain had fallen on them in Honduras. They had broken into her home and stolen highly classified information. They had been a step ahead of the organization for months.

It was that boy, Jake, who had caused the most trouble. It was hard not to admire his determination, and at times she had felt something almost like affection for him. But she also despised him. He had stood over her, gloating, as his family stole her files. He had even given her that nickname, the *Snake Lady*. Marjorie was aware that it was known among the organization, and that they snickered about it behind her back.

But maybe Jake wasn't really to blame. Maybe she just wasn't up to the responsibility the council had given her. Maybe that, ultimately, was why they were about to take it away.

She entered the council chamber and again found herself alone. The other eight members attending were in hologram form – black shapes, living shadows, standing around a table.

"Councillor number nine," one of the shadows said. "Thank you for joining us."

She recognized the sneering tone and overweight shadow. It was Lord Osthwait, a pompous British aristocrat whose only achievement was leading the operation to locate the first emerald tablet in Ethiopia. That was four years ago, and they had found four others since without his direct involvement, yet he still gloated about it at any opportunity. She had never seen the man in person – the council were never in the same place physically – but she detested him, and the feeling, she knew, was mutual.

"Quite some mess you have in Beijing," the shadow figure said.

Bite your tongue. Watch your words. It had been tough enough convincing them to let her continue after the Atlas family had invaded her home, but she hadn't been removed from the operation yet.

"It has been a difficult week," she conceded.

Lord Osthwait's shadow snorted. "Locating the Ethiopian tablet was *difficult*, but I achieved it, did I not?"

"You did. Some time ago."

"This operation has not been difficult. It has been a shambles."

"There remain positives."

"We cannot find any."

We. So they had met behind her back.

"We are in possession of five of the nine tablets," Marjorie explained. "We hope to locate another one here in the Paris catacombs by the end of the month. We will have six in total, which is—"

"Councillor number three?" Lord Osthwait interrupted. "You are responsible for the finances of this organization. How much would you estimate has been spent so far on the operation to locate the emerald tablets?"

"Tens of billions," came the reply.

"In what currency?"

"In any currency."

"Tens of billions," Lord Osthwait repeated. "And

yet we only have five of nine tablets. And how much, at a guess, would you estimate the Atlas family have spent so far in the course of their search?"

"A few thousand," Councillor number three confirmed.

"A few thousand!"

He sounded surprised, but Marjorie knew this had already been discussed. It was a script, a trap.

"A few thousand against tens of billions," Lord Osthwait continued. "And yet they have three of the tablets. Tell me, number nine, what exactly are the positives in that?"

"We expect them to come to Paris," Marjorie replied. "This is the last remaining tablet."

"You expect that, do you?"

Oh, God. She recognized that smug tone. They had new information.

"Is there something you need to tell me?" she asked.

"How much of your Beijing team's report did you read, number nine?"

"I ... I have yet to read the report fully. The family escaped. My focus has been in preparing for their possible arrival here in Paris."

"Well, had you taken the time to read the report," Lord Osthwait sneered, "you might be aware of the technology the Atlas family were using moments before their escape."

Why hadn't she looked? She'd been in such a rush that she'd forgotten to do her job.

"What technology?" she asked.

"A lexical analysis programme. Do you know why they might have been using such technology?"

"It is used for a high-level language decryption."

"Precisely. They were attempting to decipher the emerald code, with just three of the tablets. Meanwhile, we have five and are yet to read a single sign. How is that possible?"

"We ... are not the Atlas family."

"More's the pity."

The councillors chuckled like witches around a cauldron. There was no point in saying much more: it was over. Marjorie closed her eyes, trying to listen to the aria in her head, the seamstress singing about her love, far away from this place and these people.

"We have to assume that the family succeeded with the decipherment," Lord Osthwait continued. "And they have a clue to where the tablets lead, to the Hall of Records left behind by the lost civilization. So it seems that they know considerably more than we do. While we, with all of our tens of billions, know absolutely nothing. More than ever, the Atlas family must be stopped."

"I will devise a plan to—"

"No."

And, just like that, she was done.

This organization had taken everything from her. She had given them her whole life. She wanted to roar at them, to insist they'd have to forcibly remove her from this place. But when she finally opened her mouth, she couldn't think of a single thing to say.

"I am assuming control of this operation," Lord Osthwait continued, "by unanimous council consent. I am instigating an open hunt on the Atlas family, as I did to locate the Ethiopian tablet. Are you aware of the term 'open hunt'?"

"I ... I am."

"It is very simple, really," Lord Osthwait continued. "So far we have relied on our mercenaries to capture the Atlas family, and professional treasure hunters to search for the tablets. Now we will use the hunters to track the family. Four hours ago, every hunter on our books received the same communiqué: locate and catch the Atlas family. The reward is a quarter of a billion dollars for each family member, dead or alive."

"But ... you can't."

"We can't? We have spent ten times that so far, and still they are ahead of us. Should we catch them, we shall have their clues to locating the Hall of Records. A billion dollars is a small price to pay for such a gain."

She knew it made sense. Most treasure hunters were glorified thieves; there was little honour among them. They were skilled trackers, and stood a far better chance of finding the family than the organization's mercenaries. Only, how would they know where to start looking?

"There was something else, wasn't there," she asked. "In the report?"

"Indeed," Lord Osthwait confirmed. "The family were seen purchasing train tickets to Lhasa, in Tibet. Security footage shows them boarding the train in Beijing."

"Tibet?' Marjorie said, thinking aloud.

Her mind raced, joining up dots, seeking information from mental files. Something occurred to her, something that might be very important to locating the family, but Lord Osthwait spoke first. He tried to sound professional, bored even, but he failed to hide the delight in his next words.

"I am sorry, Marjorie, but this is now a private council meeting. Would you please leave?"

7

Things were pretty tense for the next two days, even though all we did was sit on a train. We stayed together in our sleeper cabin, jumping every time the train jolted, and flinching at each shout from a steward.

"We need to calm down," Dad insisted, although his knee was twitching in a way that suggested he wasn't at all calm. The Snake Lady had tracked us to one spot in a city of twenty million people, so we had to assume she was still on our tail.

"Jake, you're sure you destroyed our old passports?" Dad asked.

"Burned them all," I replied.

"Jane, you have the new ones? And the travel visas?"

Mum tapped her rucksack, where she'd stashed our new identities. We often travelled under assumed names, with fake passports sent by our friend Sami, who built gadgets for our missions. We'd been the Brown family, the Von Dorns, the Davidsons... Over the past six months Mum had dyed her hair a dozen different colours, and Dad had worn wigs and different glasses, even a weird prosthetic nose. I used hoodies to hide my face, but Pan always refused to wear disguises. She moaned that she wore what she wore and if the bad guys didn't like it, they could get stuffed.

Sometimes it's hard to remember that my sister is a genius.

Mum had taken her lucky necklace off. She wound its chain around her hand and clutched its amulet in her palm. "We're the Zolotaya family now," she told us. "From Russia."

"Wait." Pan pulled a headphone from her ear. "We don't speak Russian."

"Your father and I do," Mum said.

I wasn't surprised. I'd grown used to discovering new things about our parents – languages they spoke, vehicles they drove, weapons they could handle – skills they'd picked up long before me and Pan were born.

"Pandora," Dad asked, "did you swap our train tickets?"

Pan nodded, shoving the headphone back in her ear. "Some American family is in our cabin, and we're in theirs," she said.

All Pan had to do at the station was find a target family, bump into whichever of them was holding their tickets, and drop ours too. The swap was made, big apologies all round.

We'd watched our backs, done everything right. We should have been relaxing. But still we sat on the edge of our bunks, knees twitching faster with every passing minute.

The train gathered speed, leaving the city and heading into the countryside. Outside, house lights grew fewer, and the night began to close in.

"We should get some sleep," Mum suggested. "We have a forty-hour train ride ahead."

"You think any of us can sleep?" Pan replied. "Where are we even going? And when are you going to tell us what that word from the tablet means?"

I tried to hide a grin. I'd wanted to ask that too, but I knew Pan would crack first.

"Kailas," Pan said. "We know you know."

Dad looked at Mum, and they had one of their wordless arguments: rolls of eyes, sighs and shrugs. I don't think Mum planned to keep it a secret for ever, and the time had come to let us know.

Dad pulled out one of our duffel bags from under his bunk and brought out a glass rectangle the size of a smartphone. It was a mini holosphere, one of the few bits of kit we'd been able to save from the Beijing headquarters, other than our smart-goggles. He laid it on the table between the bunk beds, and tapped it in three specific spots. The device came to life, projecting a hologram keyboard onto which he started typing until the image changed to a map of China. Using a finger, he traced our path west across swathes of countryside.

"We are here now, leaving Beijing."

I sat forward on the bed, following the route. It looked like we were travelling across *all* of China. Our destination was so far away that Dad had to scroll the map for several seconds to find it.

"This is Tibet," he said.

"Tibet?" Pan asked. "As in ... Tibet?"

"Yes. That word you translated, Kailas, is the name of a mountain there."

"A mountain?" I asked. "You mean in the Himalayas? So that's where we'll find the Hall of Records. Simple."

Mum sighed in a that's-a-very-disappointing-thing-to-hear kind of way. "It's never simple, Jake," she said. "You should know that by now."

"Nothing about Tibet is simple," Dad explained.

As he spoke, his fingers moved across the hologram map, zooming in and out of features in the landscape. I noticed the twinkle in his eyes; he loved these little lectures.

"Mount Everest is here. This is the border with Nepal, and this one is with India. Here's Tibet's capital, Lhasa, where this train is taking us. It's 11,450 feet above sea level, so there's far less oxygen than in most other places. The air is so thin you could get altitude sickness just walking to the shops."

"Where's Mount Kailas?" Pan asked.

"All the way over here, in the west of Tibet. There is only one road that far, and it will be guarded – if not by the People of the Snake, then the Chinese army."

"Hang on. I thought this was Tibet, not China?"

"Tibet *is* China, Jake," Pan said. "The Chinese invaded it in 1950. A lot of Tibetans fled over the Himalayas. Others fought back, but they didn't stand a chance. The rest just try to live as best as they can under Chinese occupation."

"Well, that sucks, but what's so special about Mount Kailas?"

"Everything, to millions of people," Dad replied. "Three different religions – Buddhism, Jainism and Hinduism – regard it as the place where the world began, a home of gods. To many of those people it's known as the Crystal Mountain."

"Crystal?" I asked, thinking of the coffins we'd found the emerald tablets inside, all made of gleaming carved crystal. "Why's it called that?"

"I don't know for sure," Dad said. "There are legends that the mountain contains crystal caves..."

I edged even further forward. "Does it?"

"No one would know," Dad muttered. "No one has climbed Mount Kailas."

That was weird, but good news. If no one had explored this mountain, maybe there were secrets there to be found. Just the thought of scaling a Himalayan peak made my stomach churn – I wasn't

54

good with heights – but I'd worry about that when we got there.

"So we need to find this mountain and search its caves for the Hall of Records?" I suggested.

"No one climbs Mount Kailas," Mum said. "It's sacrilegious."

"But not to us," I shot back. "We're not Hindus or Buddhists or ... that other one you said."

"That doesn't matter, Jake," Mum insisted. "We respect those faiths. Anyway, Kailas is unclimbable. Its sides are sheer walls of rock and ice. Even the world's best mountaineers say it is impossible, not that they would try. There is no way up Mount Kailas."

Dad did a sort of mumbled grunt and a slight shrug. Pan and I had spent a long time learning to decipher our parents' secret gestures. We knew this one well; Dad's way of discreetly disagreeing with Mum.

"So there is a way?" Pan asked.

"No," Mum said.

"Maybe," Dad said.

"Let's go with maybe," Pan decided. "Which way?"

"It's just a rumour, a legend," Dad replied.

"It's mumbo jumbo," Mum said.

She flapped a hand as if to swat away a fly. Mum never liked talking about things she called "mumbo jumbo" – ghosts and aliens and stuff like that. It was strange; we were risking our lives to hunt for an ancient civilization that had come long before even the Ancient Egyptians, but at least once a week Mum muttered that the whole idea was mumbo jumbo.

Dad, though, *loved* mumbo jumbo. He always tried to sound academic about it, but weird *X-Files* stuff made his eyes glimmer and caused the dimple in his chin to crease up.

"Not necessarily, Jane," he countered. "What about the Drak Terma?"

"The what?" I asked.

"In Buddhism, terma means 'hidden knowledge'," Dad said. "A terma is a record of ancient wisdom that's kept secret from the world because it's thought to be dangerous. One of these, known as the Drak Terma, is said to reveal a secret way inside Mount Kailas, to a store of ancient knowledge."

"You mean, knowledge about a lost civilization?" I asked, my pulse quickening. "That's why Kailas was written on the emerald tablet. So that's *definitely* where we'll find the Hall of Records."

Dad gave Mum another look – a raised eyebrow and a tilt of his head that signalled something like "they may be right, but I shouldn't agree, should I?"

Mum shook her head, but she couldn't dismiss it entirely. "Even if the Drak Terma does exist," she said, "no one knows where it is."

Dad made that mumbly-grunty noise again. "One person might."

Now it was Mum's shot in the tennis match of

secret looks. This one was a winner, a long hard stare as she wound her necklace so tight around her palm that her fingers turned white. They knew more than they were saying – a lot more. I was about to ask, when the train came to a sudden stop and I tumbled off my bunk. Shouts rang along the corridor, and guards marched past our cabin.

Immediately, Mum grabbed a rucksack and rooted through it for bits of kit. "John, blow the train lights," she hissed. "Everyone, put on your goggles, switch to NVG. We're going up to the train roof. We can fire a zip line from there to—"

"Wait." Pan pressed her face to the window. "It's not about us."

Further along the train, Chinese army officers were grappling with a red-faced American man in pyjamas. The guy was furious, yelling about mistaken identities. His wife and two sons huddled close by, struggling to work out if this was a nightmare.

"It's the family whose tickets I swapped with ours," Pan muttered.

In the window reflection, I saw Mum and Dad look at each other – this time there were no secret signals, just a long hard stare.

"We're safe here," Mum said, finally. "By the time they work out the mistake we'll be in Lhasa. Just keep the lights out and stay quiet."

Pan climbed back to her bunk and pulled her hood over her head, but I kept watching. As the train pulled away, the police led the distraught family to a van, the dad now in handcuffs.

"They'll be OK, right?" I asked.

"Just try to sleep, Jake," Mum replied. "Tomorrow's a big day."

8

Remember what my dad said about the air being thinner in Tibet?

It didn't mean a lot to me at the time. I mean, how can air be *thin*? You don't really think about air unless you're drowning or suffocating. Then it's all you think about, like in that tunnel in the Great Pyramid when that sand was... That doesn't matter. My point is, I don't usually think much about the air I breathe.

That changed the moment I stepped off the train. Lhasa Railway Station is 3,650 metres above sea level. I could still breathe, but each breath felt as if someone was squeezing my lungs, just slightly, like a little warning.

Along the platform, passengers pressed their hands to their chests, feeling the same discomfort. Only a few – locals, I guessed – didn't seem to notice.

"Just breathe normally," Mum said. "Give your body time to adjust. Come on."

My parents wore disguises – wigs and glasses that looked a bit silly – and they talked to each other in fluent Russian as we carried our bags towards the security check, where a line of grim-faced officials glared at us from glass booths. We were the first to approach, which wasn't very smart if our plan was to blend in.

"We're Russian," Mum hissed.

"What? I can't walk any slower than this."

"No. We're *Russian*, remember? Stop speaking English."

"Do we even *look* Russian?"

"How do Russians look, Jake?"

"I don't know, Pan! More Russian than us, I'd guess."

One of the guards beckoned us, and reached a hand through a hole in his booth.

"American?" he grunted.

We shook our heads.

"English?"

I nodded, and then shook my head. Pan gave me a shoulder nudge.

"*Rooskee*," Dad said, handing over our fake passports. "*Ya plokha gavaryoo pa angleeskee*," he added.

The guard glared at him, and then at the documents, and back and forth about a dozen times, as I grew increasingly certain that there *was* a Russian look, and it looked nothing like us.

"First time in Tibet?" he asked.

Pan and I nodded. I noticed a slight hesitation from Mum, and a glance at Dad, but they nodded too.

The guard watched us for another long moment. Then, slowly, he reached for something under his counter. He rose and opened the door to his booth.

"Step closer," he ordered.

None of us moved. My mind went into that zone again, instinctively making a plan. The man had a slight limp, so I'd go for his knee – a sharp kick, enough to take him down so we could escape.

Maybe Mum was thinking the same thing, because she edged forward. I noticed her fist curl, her jaw lock. The guard raised a strip of white silk, his grip tight on its edges, as if he might use it to strangle us. I braced myself to go for him...

The guard reached out and draped the material over Mum's head.

It was a scarf!

"Welcome to Tibet Autonomous Region," he said.

We all grinned, trying not to laugh, as the guy gave each of us a white scarf, stamped our documents and waved us through.

"What was that about?" I whispered.

"It's a *khadas*," Dad told me, under his breath. "A Tibetan prayer scarf."

As I stepped outside I had to stop myself from reaching for my smart-goggles. Tech like that would give us away, but I *really* needed sunglasses. It was cold, late winter, but crazy bright. The sky was a whole new kind of blue, pure and rich and deep. In every direction I saw mountains: grey-brown hunch-backed giants. In the high-altitude air they looked incredibly sharp, like we'd upgraded an old TV to a new plasma screen.

"It's amazing," I said.

"Wait until you see the stars at night," Dad replied.

I glanced at Pan, who threw me the same curious look. Mum and Dad had *definitely* been here before. I wanted to ask more, but we had to focus on what was going on right then. The People of the Snake might have beaten us here. They could be anywhere, around any corner.

"Just relax," Dad said.

He didn't seem relaxed. We feared we were being watched, but *everyone* was watching us: taxi drivers, pedicab riders, a scrum of tour guides waggling signs. Chinese police officers leaned against a concrete pillar topped with a bronze statue of a horse doing a four-legged jump.

The taxi driver had his foot down the whole way into Lhasa, as if he was desperate to reach a dying friend. It was annoying. We were always in a rush, fleeing from some bad guy or racing to some ancient shrine. These moments, when I actually got to see a new place, were precious. I didn't want to miss a thing.

We crossed a sleek, arched bridge over a river, and entered Lhasa, where the driver was forced to slow down to navigate narrow, mazelike streets. I leaned into the window, my excited breaths misting the glass. I saw businessmen in coffee shops, and shaven-headed monks in blood-coloured robes gathered around a street seller roasting corn.

Most of the buildings looked the same: white and square and simple. Few were higher than two storeys, which made sense. If you're surrounded by the Himalayas you don't want to boast about your size.

Only one building was taller. At first we only glimpsed it between houses, on its perch at the top of a craggy hill. Gleaming white walls rose to a bright red palace crowned with golden domes that flickered in the sun.

"The Potala," Pan breathed.

"The what?"

"The Potala Palace," she explained. "It was the home of the Dalai Lama before he fled the Chinese invasion."

"The who?"

"The Dalai Lama. You've heard of him, right?"

"Maybe?"

"Jake! He's the spiritual leader of Tibet. Sort of like the Pope for Buddhism, but less rich."

The driver braked sharply, swearing at a huge, hairy cow that blocked the road.

"Yaks," Dad said. "They're sacred to Tibetans."

"They don't seem sacred to this driver," Pan muttered.

"They're not; he's Chinese."

The driver dropped us off at the hotel and accelerated away with a screech as we stood and stared. We'd visited a few countries recently, but the hotels were always the same: "nothing fancy", as Mum put it, which meant cheap and shabby. They were usually one-star places – if they got lucky on star-grading day – where Mum and Dad thought no one would look for us. I'd fallen asleep staring at damp patches on walls and listening to mice scuttle behind bed boards. But this hotel...

"It's incredible," Pan said.

It was called the Shangri-La, and it was properly five-star. A fake Chinese gateway led to a courtyard with a marble fountain and bushes sculpted in wavy lines. Inside, the lobby was all polished wood and plush furniture. Everything seemed to shine, even the reception staff's perfect teeth.

Dad checked us in, talking in weird broken English, like it was his second language.

"How will we pay for this place?" I whispered.

"*We* won't," Mum replied.

"Eh?"

"We don't pay for our hotels, Jake."

"Eh?"

"We use the People of the Snake's money. The Snake Lady gave us their bank card when we worked for her in Honduras, remember?"

I remembered, but that was months ago.

"We *kept* using it," Mum continued. "Sami runs tracking interference on it so they can't use it to locate us. But we assume they don't notice, because they've not cancelled the account."

"Hang on," Pan said. "The People of the Snake have been *funding* us?"

"They have."

"So why have we been staying in such horrible hotels?"

"Well, for one, I don't want to raise children who only know luxury. You'll grow soft. But also, those were good places to lie low."

"*Lie low,*" I muttered. "Yeah, the mattresses were usually on the floor."

"So why are we upgrading now?" Pan asked.

"We're supposed to be Russian millionaires, so we can hardly stay in a backpacker hostel. Just don't get used to it."

I didn't want to get used to it or it would break my heart to stay anywhere else. We booked a suite, where our rooms were linked by a lounge with a colossal TV and a balcony with a view across the city. The beds were as big and bouncy as a trampoline and the bathroom had a Jacuzzi. That was exactly what I needed after the long train ride, but as soon as I ran the tap Mum yanked the plug out.

"No washing," she said.

"What? Why not?"

"Hot water weakens your circulation, which can

cause illness, which you do not want at high altitude. There's not enough oxygen to recover."

"So we don't wash?"

"You can wash your hands."

I did, and then sat for a while on the toilet. We'd only had squat loos in China, so this was proper luxury. By the time I went back into the lounge, Mum had her laptop out, and Dad had set up his holosphere on a table. They talked in low voices, scrolling through hologram web pages and discarding them with frustrated flicks.

We needed to find an ancient document – the Drak Terma – that revealed some sort of secret on Mount Kailas, maybe the Hall of Records. Only, we didn't even know if the document even existed. Dad had suggested someone here in Tibet might have a better idea, and it looked like they were working on way to find the person.

"Hang on, have you two made a plan?" I asked.

"Just some research," Mum replied, dismissively. "John, the first number is for Tibet Vista Tours."

Dad called the phone number and spoke in his fake bad English. I looked at Pan, but her shrug suggested she was equally confused as we listened to Dad book a tour of Potala Palace under our fake Russian name, Zolotaya.

"Are we going sightseeing?" Pan asked.

"Not exactly," Dad said as he hung up.

Mum gave him another number, and then

another. It was baffling; they booked us on the same tour with twenty different travel companies, giving each the same name and meeting place outside the palace.

Mum closed her laptop. "I think that's all of them," she said.

"Are you going to tell us what that was about?" Pan asked.

Mum didn't – she *never* did. Whatever was happening, it related to her past life with Dad and their work as treasure hunters before me and Pan were born. They rarely spoke about those times. Sometimes Dad would break into a story from the old days, but Mum always shut him down. I never understood why; they were the good guys in all of the stories we *had* heard. But sometimes I wondered if there were *other* stories, ones they didn't want us to hear.

"So we're booked on the same tour with every company in Tibet," Pan said. "Why?"

"It's a signal of sorts," Mum revealed.

"To the person we need to find?"

"First, let's get some rest."

Typical Mum, all mysterious. It drove Pan crazy, but I didn't mind. She wasn't blocking us out of the plan; she was just keeping her cards close to her chest for a while.

We got room service – burgers and chips – and drank more water, but the fancy hotel room lost its appeal after a couple of hours. Pan read every book on the shelves: volumes on the history of Tibet, Buddhism, and even one on Tibetan language, which I think she hoped to learn in one night. I just stared beyond the balcony, to where the Potala Palace rose above the city like a red-and-white mountain, as frustration boiled inside me. We were so close to finding out where the emerald tablets led. I didn't want to sit around a hotel room, no matter how swanky it was.

That night was nasty too. I kept waking with a dry mouth, like I'd been chewing sand. When I did sleep, I had crazy dreams. In one I was with my family in a Himalayan valley, surrounded by snow-capped mountains, looking up at Mount Kailas. The valley swarmed with military vehicles, trucks and helicopters. The People of the Snake were uncovering the mountain's secrets. I turned and saw Marjorie, the Snake Lady, right beside me, her snow-white hair lit almost orange by the sun and her ruby lips curled in a smug, victorious grin. It felt so real, the heartbreak of defeat...

I hated that woman.

I woke again and went to get more water. A curtain rustled, and I saw that the balcony door was open. I edged closer and slowly pulled back the curtain.

"Dad?"

He sat wrapped in a duvet, gazing across Lhasa, as the morning sun began to paint the rooftops pink and red. When he heard me he looked away, wiped his face on the duvet, and then turned back and smiled.

"Hey, Jakey," he said.

He only called me *Jakey* when he wanted to hide something. His eyes looked red and blurry. Was it the altitude, the lack of sleep ... or had he been crying? He slid his glasses on and stared again across the city. A flock of birds swept through a sea of mist and up past the Potala, which looked like a fairytale castle in the clouds.

"Beautiful, isn't it?" he said.

"Were you here before?" I asked.

"Yes. A long time ago."

"How long?"

"Another lifetime."

"What happened? Has it got something to do with the person we hope to meet?"

Dad didn't look at me. I sensed that he couldn't. His gaze stayed lost somewhere among the dawn-coloured roofs.

"Are you OK, Dad?" I asked.

"I will be if I get a hug."

"No way."

"Come on! One hug!"

I hugged him, and saw salty tracks on his cheeks. Suddenly I felt awkward, like I was intruding, so I left him alone and rushed back to bed.

I didn't really sleep after that. I lay awake, angry at Mum and Dad for keeping secrets. We were supposed to be a team, but it didn't always feel that way.

Maybe, though, some things weren't meant to be shared. All I knew was that this place – Tibet – held a difficult memory for my parents. I had no idea then that the story would soon involve me too, and in the worst possible way.

9

The breakfast buffet was *insane*.

I piled my plate with far more food than I could eat: pancakes and syrup, sausages and bacon, watermelon chunks and chocolate cereal. My family stared at me as I shovelled the mushed-up mix into my mouth.

"That's disgusting," Pan muttered.

"It really is," Mum agreed.

Mum had a tiny bit of toast, Pan picked at a yoghurt, and Dad downed three coffees. We all looked bleary-eyed from lack of sleep. It wasn't just the dreams that had kept us awake, but also all the water we'd had to drink to help us acclimatize. I'd needed to pee about ten times.

"What time's our tour?" I asked, between mouthfuls.

"We're not going on a tour, Jake."

I knew that; I was playing dumb to get information. "But you booked us on one with every guide in Lhasa. How will that help us find your contact?"

Dad looked at Mum, who shrugged, giving him permission to reveal more of their plan.

"The name we used to book the tours," Dad said.

"The Russian name. Zolotaya?" I asked. "That's just a made-up identity that Sami put in the passports, isn't it?"

"Keep your voice down," Mum hissed. "It's not just a random name. We gave Sami specific names for some of the documents."

"The names are signals," Pan realized. "You booked a tour with every company, so there will be twenty guides holding up a card with that name. To most people it will look like a prank, but if your contact sees it they'll recognize the name."

Dad poured himself a fourth coffee. "It's an old trick," he said. "Not one that always works."

"But who's the contact?" I asked. "And how will they know where to meet us?"

Mum dropped her toast and pushed the plate away. "Just eat up."

I wish I hadn't eaten so much. After treasure hunting, overdoing it with food is my favourite thing. But this time I had overdone overdoing it.

"Does altitude do weird things to your stomach?" I asked.

"No, Jake," Mum replied. "Fifth helpings at breakfast do. Now look sharp."

I was supposed to be looking out for signs that the People of the Snake might be watching. But it's hard when you're in a new place to look at anything other than the new place. Especially a place like Lhasa.

We walked past shoeshine boys, ear cleaners and eyebrow pluckers. Noodle stalls, hair salons, discos, and karaoke bars. Shops flogging expensive souvenirs to tourists – traditional woven carpets, turquoise and coral jewellery, jewelled Tibetan knives. There were guesthouses and teahouses and yak-steak houses. Yaks seemed big business here: there were places selling yak butter, yak cheese, even coats stuffed with yak hair. Children leaned out of windows, yelling *"Tashi delek!"* and sticking out their tongues. At first I thought they were being rude, until Pan explained.

"'Tashi delek' means blessings and good luck," she told me.

"So why are they poking their tongues out at us?" I asked.

"That's a form of respect here, Jake."

That was awesome! I continued along the street, sticking my tongue out at every local I passed. It was easy to spot the Tibetans among the tourists. They had rounder faces, which they needed for their crazy big smiles. Some of the men dressed like cowboys, in wide-brimmed hats and heavy woollen tunics called a *chuba*. Women wore layers of fur and leather, and flowerpot hats with hanging flaps.

Most of the buildings looked the same: low and whitewashed, but with crazy splashes of colour. Wooden shutters were painted with intricate patterns in bright yellow, red and green, and chains of multicoloured flags hung from roofs, like festival bunting. Every flag was covered in written prayers that were thought to rise into the sky each time they fluttered.

The decorations were amazing, but they looked ordinary compared to the Potala. Sheer whitewashed walls, dazzling in the sunlight, led up to the red and gold palace, with its fluttering flags. I'd seen hillforts before; they usually glared down in warning at a town. The Polata, though, looked like a welcome banner in the heart of the city.

Sleepy-looking sightseers clambered from tour buses in the palace forecourt, watched by suspicious Chinese army officials. As we approached, the soldiers shifted their attention to the other side of the forecourt, where a bunch of tour guides were getting into a squabble. They'd all begun to notice that their placards showed the same name: *Zolotaya.*

Pan spotted me grinning. "It's not funny, Jake," she muttered. "Those guides just lost a morning's work."

"Yeah, but for a good reason, right?"

"*Our* reason. Not theirs."

"None of them lost anything," Mum said. "We paid them all up front. Come on."

We carried on past the guides and into a warren of streets, where so many soldiers watched from rooftops that it felt like we'd entered a siege. They were on every corner too, with riot shields and machine guns. Maybe the locals were used to them, or perhaps they refused to be intimidated, because none of them seemed to notice. Everyone was too busy being religious.

Almost immediately we became part of a flow of Tibetans shuffling in the same direction through the narrow streets, all thumbing prayer beads and chanting.

"They're walking the *kora*, aren't they, Dad?" Pan asked, shouting above the noise of all the prayers.

"The what?" I asked.

"This area is called Barkor," Dad said. "It's the holiest part of Lhasa. Devout Buddhists come here to walk a route known as a *kora,* a clockwise pilgrimage around its temples."

Almost *every* building here was a temple, judging from the number of people chanting outside them. Monks in rose and saffron-coloured robes scattered petals around flagstones. Some pilgrims were on their knees praying; others ran their hands along rows of bronze drums that spun on wooden frames.

"What are those spinny things?" I asked.

"Prayer wheels," Mum replied. "Each one contains hundreds of written prayers. Each time you spin it all of the prayers are supposed to fly up to heaven."

"No one needs that many prayers, do they?"

"Buddhism is all about merit, Jake," Pan explained. "If you say enough prayers and make enough pilgrimages, you'll get reincarnated as a better person."

I kept staring, turning, trying to take it all in. One thing still seemed weird: if Buddhists were all about helping other people, why were there so many beggars? Dozens of them sat along the walls holding out pots and croaking "*Guchi, guchi...*"

"Why are there so many homeless people?" I asked.

"They're not homeless," Dad told me, "they're pilgrims. Some have spent everything they have to get here. They ask for money to get home, and other pilgrims help."

We kept moving with the pilgrims until the lanes opened to a small square outside a temple that made all the others seem like a warm-up. Everyone here was going nuts – weeping, chanting, and shuffling in circles. Some people slid on their stomachs along the ground, thrusting their arms towards the temple. The paving stones were polished to a shine from all the people sliding around.

I hadn't known religion could be done at such volume. The train-carriage rattle of spinning prayer wheels and the constant chanting were so loud we could barely hear ourselves speak.

"This is the Jokhang Temple," Pan said. "It's the holiest place in Buddhism."

The building was a bit bigger than the others: two big white square blocks and a smaller red one in the middle. But it was nothing grand, considering its importance. Two gold statues of deer guarded an entrance draped with banners and prayer flags.

"So why are we here?" I asked.

Pan and I looked at our parents, thinking they might finally tell us what this was all about. But they just stared at the temple with glazed eyes, like they were at a funeral. Dad reached out to take Mum's hand, but she snapped it away and suddenly she was all business again.

"Let's get on with this," she said.

I still had no idea what *this* was, only that we were in this madness. I was beginning to get annoyed; our parents kept banging on about how we had to act like a team and then deliberately kept us in the dark.

I guess Pan felt the same, because as we followed our parents into the temple she mouthed a few words that I can't write here. Mum and Dad seemed to know what they were doing, but as I followed them through the gloomy entrance, I began to get a bad feeling about this place.

10

Our parents led us deeper into the temple, past a huge bronze prayer wheel. Pilgrims shuffled clockwise around it, turning the drum by a handle at its base. Some were going round several times, grinning like kids in a revolving door. The deeper we went into the temple, the thicker the air grew with smoke from incense and yellow candles in racks against wall.

"That smoke reeks," Pan muttered.

"Yak butter candles," Dad replied. "You'll smell that a lot in Tibet."

Inside, we joined a throng of pilgrims on a *kora* route around pillared chapels with so many drapes and banners that it seemed like we were walking through a series of tents. Statues of the Buddha watched us from altars, their wide candle-lit eyes glaring as if they'd just caught us stealing one of the pilgrims' prayer beads.

The place was absolutely pulsing. Pilgrims chanted, whispered, gasped and sobbed. Beads clicked, drums banged and cymbals clashed. Some pilgrims were on the ground, dragging themselves around the chapels on their bellies. Yak butter smoke drifted through sunlight shafts from high windows.

It was a really interesting place, but I was so annoyed with my parents for being secretive that I was on the verge of walking off, until Dad suddenly stopped. He'd led us into a niche off one of the chapels, the only altar that didn't seem to feature on the pilgrimage route. There was no statue here, just about a hundred yak butter candles flickering in tiered rows.

My parents exchanged another weird look, and Mum sighed so heavily that every one of the candles flickered.

"You do it," she told Dad.

"Do what?" Pan seethed. "This is infuriating. Tell me, *I'll* do it."

"Be quiet, Pandora," Mum snapped.

There was a touch of "or else" about that, so Pan just huffed. Mum and Dad didn't seem to hear as they gazed at the altar and its racks of candles.

"I've forgotten the sequence," Dad said.

"John, you can't have."

"It was fourteen years ago, Jane."

"Fine, I'll do it."

All Pan and I could do was watch as Mum leaned

towards the altar and blew out six candles up and down the racks. Foul-smelling yak butter smoke rose in columns, causing her to splutter. I still had no idea what was going on, but Pan had sussed it out.

"That sequence of candles was a code, wasn't it?" she breathed.

Dad checked that no one was watching. "A hatch just opened under the altar," he whispered. "We need to go through, hands and knees, one by one. Jane, you first. Ready?"

"But you taught us to never to go through a secret entrance unless you know what's on the other side," I said.

"That was not in your training."

"Actually it was, John," Mum muttered.

"Was it? Well, I'm changing the rule. It's OK to do that if your parents tell you to."

"That's a terrible rule," Pan said.

"Well, it's *the* rule now. Are you ready?"

"What's the big deal, though?" I asked. "We've been through secret hatches before. And secret doors and secret tunnels and secret other things. Why's this one more secret that all those other secrets? It's needlessly mysterious."

"Very needlessly," Pan agreed. "And not even that mysterious. It's a secret hatch. Ooh, big deal."

"Jane, go!" Dad hissed.

Mum vanished, dropping and diving through the drape that hung down in front of the altar. Pan went next, then me. I rose into a small chamber with just enough light to see a wooden spiral of steps twisting up into darkness.

Dad crawled through after me, then sprang up into a slightly unnecessary action pose. "Everyone OK?" he asked.

"You could have just said there were stairs here," I replied.

"*So* needlessly mysterious," Pan mumbled.

Dad led the way up, our footsteps echoed into the darkness. I don't know what I expected to find at the top: a secret hideout, maybe, or a trap, or *something*. Instead there was ... nothing.

"*Torch,*" Dad whispered.

His goggles shone a super-lumen beam around a wood-panelled room that was totally empty other than a rack of candles that didn't look like they had ever been lit. A slim opening led to a corridor and more darkness.

Dad touched Mum's hand, but she snatched it away and gripped her amulet. This room meant something to them. I was about to ask what, when a creak echoed from along the corridor.

"Someone's coming," Pan whispered.

There was another noise now too, a sliding sound that, together with the creaky floorboards, sounded like a groaning old man dragging a sack.

It was just a beggar, whispering "*Guchi, guchi*" to ask for coins. The person slid along the ground, face hidden under an avalanche of shawls and robes. A calloused hand reached out, and unhealthy-looking yellow eyes peered from under the flaps of a flowerpot hat.

"Please," the beggar croaked, "help me stand."

Pan reached to help the beggar up. Mum shot forward, as if she'd been zapped with electricity.

"No, stop!" she cried.

The frail hand snatched hold of Pan's wrist. Pan didn't have time to scream before the beggar was standing up, twisting her arm, while the person's other hand whipped out a knife and held it to my sister's neck.

I could just see enough of the beggar to tell it was a woman. She looked Tibetan, with a face like old leather. Her yellow eyes grew wider, glaring. Her voice was as rough as sandpaper.

"Back off. Don't make a move."

She twisted Pan's arm tighter, causing my sister to cry out. I was about to rush at her, but Dad held me back.

"It's OK, Jake," he insisted.

I shook him off. "*OK*? She's got a knife to Pan's throat!"

I threw the crazy woman my fiercest glare. "I don't know who you are, lady, but if you harm one hair on her head, all the prayer wheels in Tibet won't forgive what I'll do to you."

A gold tooth glinted from the shadow of the beggar's hat. She was smiling.

"He really is your son, Jane," she hissed.

"You *know* this lady?" Pan screamed.

Mum moved slightly forward, hands raised in surrender. "Hello, Takara," she said. "Thank you for coming. Please could you let go of my daughter? We are here to talk, nothing more."

"The last time you promised me that," the woman shot back, "a lot more happened than just talking. Or have you forgotten?"

"We've not forgotten."

"So why are you here? I saw your little signal with the guides."

"We need information."

"I don't help treasure hunters any more. I'm a pilgrim now. "

Dad edged forward too, pushing me gently back as he did. "Fourteen years, Takara. That whole time you've been here?"

Her golden tooth gleamed brighter in his torch light. "Perhaps you think forgiveness for what we did comes easier than that."

"We gave up treasure hunting too," Mum said. "After..."

Her voice broke, and she clutched her amulet.

"*Say it*," the woman snarled. "Say what we did. Say it or I'll cut her throat."

I was trying hard to keep up. This woman had worked with my parents here in Tibet, but something had gone wrong. She'd stayed here ever since, shuffling around the city to seek forgiveness for ... something.

But even as I listened, my eyes shot around the

chamber. I'd gone into that zone again, instinctively making a plan to save my sister. The floorboards were loose and old; if I stamped on the right one, its other end would knock the rack of candles into the woman. It might distract her, give me a chance to grab Pan.

But again Dad seemed to know what I was thinking. He stepped in front of me, blocking my path to the lady and my sister.

"You're not going to hurt anyone, Takara," he said. "So put that knife away and let's talk. Do you think we want to be in this place any more than you do? It was the only way we could find you. Besides, you didn't have to come. You want to know why we're here as much as we need to tell you, so let's stop this nonsense and just talk."

The woman threw Dad a long, hard glare. I was about to burst past him to try my plan, when the knife finally slid away from Pan's neck.

Pan staggered forward, glaring at Mum and then Dad through wild hair. She was furious, and not because of the knife. Our parents had always told us they retired when we were born, but this woman said they were here fourteen years ago – a year before Mum got pregnant. *That* was when they'd stopped.

They had lied to us. They'd given up for another reason.

"What the hell is going on?" Pan gasped.

11

We met the beggar in a restaurant close to the Jokhang Temple, a grubby place for backpackers called the *Hard Yak Café*. Students with dreadlocks and beaded necklaces eyed us over flat whites and travel guides. They looked baffled to see an average-looking family sitting with a local pilgrim.

I sat with Mum, Dad and Pan, squeezed into one side of the table, while Takara eyed us from the other side. Her face was as dirty as the café floor, and her forearms were all muscle and wire. That made sense if she'd spent fourteen years crawling around the ground on a pilgrimage.

Mum ordered heaps of Tibetan food – steamy little dumplings called *momos*, fried yak jerky and tasty-looking doughnut balls made of a flour called *tsampa*. I was up for trying it all, but I didn't get a chance. As soon as it arrived, the crazy lady pulled the plates to her and began to scoff the lot.

The café owner, who had the biggest smile I'd ever seen, poured us cups of yak butter tea. *That* was totally disgusting. It tasted like bacon-flavoured milk, and to make it worse the guy hovered nearby with the pot. Every time I took a sip – just to be polite – he topped up the cup, so the torture never ended.

Takara wiped her mouth with one of her shawls. "So, why are you here?"

"Because we need to be," Mum replied.

"That's not good enough," the woman grunted.

"Does it really matter to you?" Dad asked.

With a dirty nail she tried to pick a bit of dumpling from her gold tooth. "You know that others have tried get me back into the game, to help them find artefacts. I refused them all. Why should you be any different?"

"Because we're trying to do the right thing," Mum said.

"What do you know about the *right thing*?"

Mum sighed, rubbed her eyes. "Takara, do you really think after everything that happened, we'd come out of retirement, come back here, if it wasn't important?"

Again the woman grinned, although her smile had no joy in it. "Do your darling children know what you did here all those years ago?" she hissed.

"We know," Pan said.

It was a lie, but we had to act like a team. "That's

why we're here," my sister added. "To make amends."

Takara slurped yak butter tea, waved for the manager to top up her cup, and then shoved two more dumplings in her mouth. "I don't think you really know anything," she mumbled. "What is it you want, anyway?"

"The Drak Terma," Dad told her.

She stopped eating, her mouth still stuffed with dumpling, as if her jaw had frozen. She stared at us one by one, seeking some sign that she had misheard.

"You're joking?" she asked, finally.

"No," Dad told her. "Before... Before you retired, you were the world's expert in esoteric Buddhist literature. Does the Drak Terma exist?"

Takara swallowed a last bit of food, then pushed her plate away. Either she was finally full or she'd just lost her appetite. "Mount Kailas," she said. "That's not where you're going, is it?"

"We have a clue that points in its direction," Mum explained. "Or, rather, to some sort of secret that the mountain holds. We need to know what the Drak Terma says about it."

"This secret," Pan pressed, "is about a catastrophe that wiped out an ancient civilization. It may happen again and kill millions."

Takara sneered, as disbelieving as she was unimpressed. "What catastrophe?"

"We don't know yet," Dad said. "But there is an organization that want to find out too, and hide the information. They want to manage this disaster to control the world's population. They are coming here and they will destroy this place to find what they're after. But not if we find it first."

She gave another derisive snort, but there was something new in her yellow eyes – fear, maybe, or at least concern.

"Have you seen all the soldiers around this city?" she asked. "The Chinese government is not going to allow some organization to come here and—"

"They're more powerful than any government."

I was the one that spoke, but Takara's eyes stayed on my parents. Whatever their history was together, she believed what they said.

"It sounds like you owe this place a debt," Pan added. "You can settle it by helping us stop those people from tearing Tibet apart and letting millions die."

Takara sat staring into the last of her yak butter tea, as if seeking answers in its curdled surface. She gestured to the manager for a top-up, and drank the whole cup before she finally looked again at my mum.

"The Drak Terma exists," she said.

"Where, Takara?"

"In a monastery."

"Which one?"

"First, you must make me a promise. You will ask the monks for permission to view it. If they refuse, that is your answer. You will respect their decision and leave."

"Of course," Mum replied.

I sat up, glaring at Mum – was she crazy? We needed to see that document no matter what the monks decided. Maybe Mum knew that I'd protest, because she spoke again quickly.

"You have my word, Takara. You have *all* of our words."

She and Mum held the longest stare, like they were having a blinking contest, and then Takara waved for the manager to top up her drink again.

"Very well," she agreed. "I will draw you a map. But there is something else you should know."

She slid a hand into her shawl and dug out a crumpled sheet of paper. A crooked, glinting smile cracked across her face as she slid the page across the table.

"You're popular," she said.

Dad's glasses slipped down his nose as he read the sheet, but he didn't nudge them back. "You were sent this?" he asked.

"I still receive certain communications from the treasure-hunting community."

Mum snatched the paper. As she read it her fingers tightened, crumpling the page even more. "My God," she breathed.

"What is it?" Pan asked.

"You were wrong that the People of Snake are coming after you," Takara snarled. "It's far worse than that. They have called an open hunt on you."

"Is that bad?" I asked.

Her grin spread wider than ever, and her golden tooth gleamed, giving her the look of a jack-o'-lantern.

"Bad barely touches it," she said. "You're in a whole new world of trouble now."

12

It was incredible how quickly we left Lhasa. I barely had time to buckle my seatbelt and squabble with Pan for space before buildings and bridges were replaced by valleys and mountains.

The road followed a river, and then we drove into a landscape slashed with valleys of shattered grey rock. Occasionally, when the hills parted, we caught glimpses of a much steeper skyline – jagged snow-covered peaks jutting through far-off cloud.

After a couple of hours of driving the only signs of life were a few whitewashed farm houses, the odd shaggy yak and dusty, red-cheeked children who scampered along the side of the road yelling *"Tashi delek"* and sticking out their tongues. I leaned out of the window of our hired jeep and *tashi-delek*ed back until Mum snapped at me, as if one of the kids might be a hunter seeking the reward on our heads.

Mum hadn't said much since we'd met Takara. An open hunt had been declared on us. Every professional treasure hunter in the world had been offered the same reward: a quarter of a billion dollars for each of us, dead or alive. But every time I tried to ask about it, Mum cut me off with the same reply: "It's nothing to worry about".

That would have been reassuring if she wasn't acting like there was a *lot* to worry about. As we drove she kept instructing her smart-goggles to switch from infrared view to thermal camera to zoom as she scanned the hillsides for danger.

"We're too exposed here," she muttered. "These valleys are too wide, John."

She said that as if there was something Dad could do about it. I sat forward and peered through the windscreen. The valleys were actually narrowing, the steep grey slopes closing in on either side.

"Do you think someone is watching us?" I asked.

"No, I do not think we are in any danger at all," Mum replied.

"What about Kyle and Veronika?"

In Honduras we'd clashed with a couple of hunters called Kyle and Veronika Flutes. We'd stolen their treasure, blasted them with stinging bullet ants and caused one of them to be attacked by a wild jaguar. They had good reason to come after us, even without the reward.

"Well, yes," Mum conceded, "I think they might be tempted. But no one else."

"Because all the others are probably somewhere else looking for treasure?" Pan asked.

"Exactly."

"Treasure worth a billion dollars?"

"I... No, that's unlikely."

"So why wouldn't they come after us instead?" I wondered.

"Well, yes, it's possible some will reason that," Mum agreed.

"Is it possible they *all* might?" Pan said.

"I suppose."

"How quickly could they get here?"

"Very quickly," Dad added. "If they were already in Asia."

"Could some be here already?" I asked

"Yes. That's possible."

"So, let me get this straight," Pan summarized. "There could be any number of treasure hunters coming after us, and they all might be here already? Didn't this start with you telling us everything was fine?"

"Everything is fine!" Mum barked. "Just sit back, will you?"

I wasn't so worried, not then, anyway. We were headed to a remote monastery two hundred miles west of Lhasa, where Takara had told us the Drak Terma was kept hidden, and no else knew our destination. To be honest, the whole open hunt thing hadn't had much of an impact on me.

Which, looking back, was really dumb.

The road grew steep as we zigzagged up to a pass at the end of the valley. To one side was a steep rock wall, to the other an almost sheer drop that really freaked me out. Each time we turned so the drop was on my side, I leaned across the seat into Pan as if my weight might otherwise tip us off the edge. My sister screamed and whacked me, Mum snapped at us and Dad yelled that he was trying to concentrate on the road. To make things worse, parts of the path were strewn with rocks that had tumbled from higher up. As Dad steered around them, I swear the jeep's tyres nudged over the edge of the road.

"You're going to kill us, Dad! Mum, I think you should drive."

"Sit back, Jake!"

"Just let me out, I'll meet you at the top of the pass."

"If you want to get out of the car, that's fine by me."

"No, Pandora, it is not fine. Everyone be quiet."

"Great, I'll just sit in silence while we fall off a mountain. Look, it just happened again! Are you *trying* to kill us, Dad? That's it, isn't it, you're after the reward! Steer *away* from the edge. *Away*, like this."

"Jake, don't you dare touch the steering wheel! Although, John, we were quite close to the edge just then..."

We drove down to another valley. Around us the hills were so high that I had to lean down just to see to their tops. Fractured grey slopes rose to wavy ridges speckled with white. I thought it was snow, but my smart-goggles showed structures of small stone steeples with golden peaks that gleamed against the deep blue Tibetan sky.

"Are those monasteries?" I asked.

"No, they're *chortens*," Pan explained. "Buddhist memorials. They contain the ashes of holy men."

Tibet must have had a lot of holy men, because I saw at least a hundred of those chorten things as we continued along one valley and down another. Shadows stretched and the mountains changed from slate grey to pastel pink as the sun sank low over the ridges. The temperature was changing too, a creeping cold that we felt even inside the jeep. I didn't much fancy going outside, but our ride ended halfway along the valley, where the road was blocked by the debris from an avalanche. Dad parked the jeep behind the rise of boulders.

"Are we near the monastery?" I asked.

"As close as we can get by car," he replied. "It's a ten-hour hike from here."

I peered in each direction along the valley. "Which way?"

Dad pointed the only way I hadn't looked: straight up the mountain. "That way."

"We go light," Mum said. "Take only what you need."

"Going light" was a phrase I'd come to dread. It made sense, especially at high altitude, to carry as little as we could, to preserve our strength. But it meant no luxuries – no chocolate bars, no pillows, and coffin-size tents for sleeping. Basically, it meant we were grumpy all the time.

We'd been in a rush to leave Lhasa, where Mum had claimed we were sitting ducks, and get to the mountains (where we still seemed like sitting ducks, only with fewer places to hide). But we'd had time to gather a few supplies. We'd found a sports store and kitted ourselves out with trekking gear: boots, rucksacks, tents and hiking trousers. None of it was high-tech, but at least we wouldn't be trekking into the Himalayas in jeans and trainers.

Mum gave us one of her safety lectures as we each packed a rucksack with the things we'd need for the hike.

"Stick together," she insisted. "Watch your step, focus on the ground ahead of you, never switch off or daydream. Don't think these mountains are harmless just because they're not steep."

I gazed up the slope we were about to climb, an almost vertical mass of broken rock and scree.

"Not steep?" I asked.

There should be a word between "hill" and "mountain". It doesn't seem right to call these mountains, compared to some of the peaks I'd soon see in Tibet, but they weren't just hills either. Hills are gentle, grassy things criss-crossed with footpaths. These were grumpy, ugly beasts with no paths at all. Climbing them at high altitude taught me there should be a new word for "knackering" too.

The higher we hiked, the more I became convinced that I could taste the lack of oxygen, like it had a flavour I was desperately missing. My breaths grew shallower, and raspy.

Dad must have heard how frantic my breathing had become because as he reached to help me up some rocks, he lifted me with one hand, plonked me down on a ledge, and sat beside me.

"Breathe calmly," he said. "The worst thing you can do is panic."

Mum agreed that we should take a rest, and we pulled off our rucksacks and sat together. We sipped water and watched a huge bird sweep up through the dusk, its wings the size of ironing boards. Dad slapped on his smart-goggles and watched it glide back across the valley.

"That's a Himalayan griffon vulture," he said.

It was the first animal I'd seen outside of Lhasa, apart from yaks, and it seemed weirdly out of place. Until then the landscape had been lifeless, the mountains eerily still, as if we were explorers on another planet. But I sensed that this place was far from dead. Maybe I was being paranoid, but it really felt like we were being watched...

By the time we reached the ridge, my lungs felt like they had shrunken to the size of raisins, and my legs as if they'd been pumped with petrol and set on fire. Then, suddenly, the pain was replaced by what I can only describe as pure joy. I wiped sweaty hair from my eyes and stared at the most spectacular view I've ever seen.

Ahead, the landscape rippled with valleys like those we'd driven along, scattered with red and gold from the setting sun. Beyond them, the horizon was sharp and fanged where a range of mountains – *real* mountains, the scary, snowy, super-steep ones – snarled up through pink cloud. Ice walls and glaciers reflected the dusk, so they looked like bonfires, pulsing and glowing as the sun dipped to kiss their peaks.

"The Himalayas," Pan breathed.

"Which one is Mount Kailas?" I asked.

"We can't see it from here," Dad replied. "It's further west."

Mount Kailas must have been *seriously* far away, because it seemed like I could see the whole world from that ridge.

"Come on," Mum said. "We'll camp in the valley down there."

It sounds strange, but going down the other side of the mountain was almost tougher than climbing up. The surface was so broken that it was difficult to find a footing. Our boots slipped in scree, causing us to slide. It took over an hour to reach the valley, and another twenty minutes for our parents to agree on the best place to camp. By then the sun had vanished behind the mountains, as darkness swallowed the valley.

We pitched our two tents in torchlight, and Dad cooked dinner on a little gas stove. There was no wood for a campfire, which was a bummer because it was freezing. Even wrapped in our coats and cocooned in sleeping bags, we shivered. There was no wind, just a penetrating coldness seeping through the layers.

Dad made some sort of stew, but my hands trembled so much I could barely hold the bowl. In the end Mum fed me like a toddler. She kept glancing at Dad and muttering "We weren't prepared for *this*," in a way that said "*You* didn't prepare for this."

You might wonder why we weren't in our tents, but there was a reason to stay outside, for a short time at least. Remember my dad mentioned the stars?

It was most amazing night sky ever. Away from lights, and high up where the air was clear, it was as if the entire universe was crammed above the valley. The night blazed with spirals and clusters, and the great smear of the Milky Way. As Mum and Dad planned our route to the monastery, Pan and I lay with our rucksacks as pillows. I'd never even seen a shooting star before, but that night we spotted dozens, silver scratches that caused us to point and gasp.

"Think how meaningless we are right now," Pan muttered. "We're all just dust in space."

She always got deep at times like that. I knew what she meant, but I sometimes suspected she was quoting lyrics from one of her heavy metal bands.

"Yeah, whatever, sis."

"I'm serious, Jake. Really, what's the point in any of this? Our treasure hunts, beating the People of the Snake. In the cosmic scale of things, who really cares?"

"Maybe try not to think about the cosmic scale of things?"

"I just don't know that it matters."

"OK, but if we're gonna do something that doesn't matter, it might as well be stopping an evil organization from hiding knowledge of a mass catastrophe that might kill millions. Better than watching YouTube videos of cats, right?"

"*Might* kill millions, Jake. We don't really know what this is all about. You're so convinced that we're right and the People of the Snake are wrong."

"Are you crazy? The Snake Lady tried to kill us. You remember that, don't you?"

"Of course I remember!"

She punched me in the arm, hard enough to suggest she remembered that day more often that she'd like.

"I'm not saying she's nice," she added. "It's just... So far on this mission, we've ruined two of China's most important archaeological sites. We may as well have taken a bulldozer to the Great Wall for the hat trick. And now we're looking for a secret way into Mount Kailas, even though that's against the religion of a billion people. Are we certain it's all worth it?"

"If that's what it takes to stop her winning."

"Is that what this is all about to you? Beating the Snake Lady? What about the relics? What about saving the world?"

I didn't reply; she was being really annoying. What we were doing mattered, and the truth is I didn't care about the things we destroyed along the way. I didn't *want* to ruin them, but that was the price to pay to stop the People of the Snake. Ultimately, people would understand.

Grumpy from the cold and the argument, I crawled into our tiny tent and curled up to sleep. Mum was on watch and Dad was on a sleep shift, snoring so loudly that any hunter within five valleys could have heard. Pan and I slept top-to-toe; my head was by the tent door and the biting cold. Muttering curses, I slid deeper into my sleeping bag and shivered myself to sleep.

13

I woke up.

Something wasn't right.

Even half-asleep, I knew. It was that sixth sense I had for danger, a part of me that was always alert. I shifted up on my elbows, listening. Pan was asleep, sunken into her sleeping bag. I could still hear Dad snoring, but farther away now, where I guessed he'd fallen asleep on his watch.

I grabbed my smart-goggles and slid them on.

"Thermal," I whispered.

My view changed to a thermal map of my surroundings – a grey haze broken by glowing orange blobs of biological heat signatures: Pan beside me and Mum sleeping in her tent. A third blob at the edge of our camp was Dad napping through his watch, but there was a fourth too. Beyond the camp, something was moving down the side of the mountain. Something large. I lay stone-still, watching the shape crouch low and then continue its silent stalk towards us.

"Pan," I hissed.

If I tried to wake her she might snap at me, and whoever was out there would hear us. The only advantage I had was that the person wasn't being as sneaky as they thought.

Think, Jake!

Outside, the orange blob stopped again and moved again. If it was a hunter, they'd have night-vision goggles. I could dazzle the person with a torch beam to give me time to wake my parents.

With a shaky hand I opened the tent. The sound of the zip was amplified by the night, so it seemed as if I was revving an engine.

The orange blob continued its slow approach, now ten metres from the camp. Its heat signature was incredibly bright, as if the person wasn't affected at all by the vicious cold.

Fear filled me with an adrenaline rush. I slid my legs out of my sleeping bag and tried to get into a position where I could pounce from the tent...

The orange blob was in the camp.

It was going for my parents' tent.

I braced myself, tensing my legs, totally focused – and then burst from the tent, like a sprinter out of the starting blocks. Only, I tripped on my rucksack, so my charge became a stumble. I yelled *"Torch!"* and glimpsed bright, startled eyes reflecting in the whirling light as I tumbled to the ground. Rolling over, I swept my light in frantic circles around the campsite.

I saw nothing, no one.

"Thermal," I rasped.

I turned again and again, scanning the area. There was something high on the ridge, but probably just an animal; no one could have moved up the mountain that fast. So where was the invader?

Dad staggered from his lookout, rubbing his eyes.

"Someone was here," I wheezed.

"Where, Jake?"

"Here. *Right here.*"

Like me, he used his thermal camera to scan the mountains. "There's nothing there. No one could have been here; it's impossible."

"And yet there was," Mum said.

She slid from her tent, pulling on her coat. I was surprised she believed me so readily over Dad. Unless...

"You saw it too?" I asked.

"I didn't know you were awake," she said. "I only knew your father wasn't." She glared at Dad in a we'll-talk-about-this-later sort of way. "But, yes, I saw the heat signature approach."

Pan was awake now too, her head poking from the tent. Her eyes were wide and full of fear. "So who was it? A hunter?"

"It wasn't moving like a hunter," I muttered. "More like an animal. A bear, maybe?"

Mum zipped up her coat and pulled a balaclava down over her face.

"I'll take the next watch."

There was no way she was letting Dad stay on lookout, although I don't think she understood who, or what, had invaded our camp. She only knew what I knew: something was in the mountains. Something was out there in the dark, watching.

14

Well, I didn't sleep much *that* night.

By the time I crawled out of my tent, the sun was peeking over the top of the ridge, reaching into the valley and thawing the frost. My breath still came in clouds, but my fingers began to tingle, sensing the morning warmth, excited.

Dad made porridge and we sat looking along the valley at the tangle of mountains beyond, and their gleaming white crowns. Breathing felt a little easier now, but that didn't mean the lack of oxygen was no longer dangerous. Mum boiled water from a stream and insisted we drank a pint each as we broke camp.

I won't tell you loads about that day's hike, other than that it was stupidly hard – up and over three passes, and then down a crazy long valley – and that something about it wasn't *right*.

I couldn't shake that creepy feeling from the night.

Something was watching us.

Mum was on full-alert mode all day. She'd trained us in military hand signals so we could react silently in danger, but I hadn't memorized them like Pan, and kept getting them wrong. I'd drop to the ground when she warned us to freeze, or turn and run when she was signalling all-clear. Mum never saw anything anyway – just prayer flags flapping in the wind, or weird-shaped rocks. At times I wondered what she was looking for. Hunters? Or did she fear that something else had been in our camp the night before?

We hiked all day as the sun wandered over the valley, stopping only for yak butter sandwiches, which were disgusting. The stuff stayed on my breath, so I tasted it again with each gasp as I trudged up and down the slopes. We fell over a lot and helped one another up. Dad was in charge of directions, but he barely looked at the map Takara had drawn. It seemed like he had an inbuilt compass. I told him that, but he replied, "No, Jake, I have an *actual* compass."

It was only as the sun began to sink again over the ridges that we caught our first glimpse of where we were headed.

"*Whoa,*" Pan breathed.

That about summed it up.

The monasteries in Lhasa had been fairly ordinary white buildings. This one was white too, a dozen small square chambers, but they were not ordinary. They clung like bird nests to a cliff at the end of the valley, linked by rock ledges and rope bridges. The scene looked like something from a fantasy film, a place where sorcerers lived. It seemed impossible – how could those buildings stick to the mountainside? Did anyone live there?

"Is that where Takara said they keep the Drak Terma?" I asked.

Dad nodded, checking the map. "It's a monastery called Yerpa Gompa. Very few people from outside Tibet have ever seen it. It is not exactly on the tourist trail."

"Yerpa Gompa," Pan said. "What does that mean?"

"A gompa is an isolated monastery, or a fort built to protect something."

"Protect what?" I asked.

Dad shrugged. "Maybe we'll find out."

15

Black-headed gulls swooped through the last of the day's light as we trekked up the path from the valley to the monastery of Yerpa Gompa. As we climbed we saw wooden stilts propping its chambers into the hillside, flagpoles and hanging banners, prayer wheels and chortens. Orange lights glowed from windows, silhouetting tiny shaven heads watching us approach.

"Will they let us in?" Pan asked.

"Of course," Dad replied. "There are few things more important to a monk than hospitality."

"So they'll show us the Drak Terma?"

"Ah, that I can't say. One of those more important things is secrecy."

The route to the monastery was so steep in places that we had to scramble on our hands and knees around slabs of rock etched with prayers. Higher up, lanterns lined the route, flickering and hissing cones of fire. They looked like gas lights.

"Where's the gas coming from?" Pan asked.

Dad crouched to inspect one of the lanterns, felt the rocks around it, and peered up the cliff above the monastery chambers. "Must be from beneath this mountain," he guessed. "Looks like they've tapped into a natural gas reserve. Clever."

A hollow blast echoed down the slope, a deep bass that caused the lanterns to tremble. It sounded like a monster had woken in its cave.

"What was that?" Pan gasped.

"A long horn," Mum said.

"Should we be worried?"

"Not at all. They are welcoming us."

The path ended at a gateway painted in crazy colours, like school kids had decorated it for a class project. We were greeted by two crimson-robed monks in flip-flops. This was some of the toughest terrain in the world and they got around in *flip-flops*. And they couldn't stop smiling.

We returned the smiles, which wasn't easy after that hike, and said "tashi delek" a lot. Prayer wheels tinkled gently in the wind as the monks draped prayer scarves over our heads and ushered us into Yerpa Gompa.

They led us along a passage between two of the stone chambers, which were brightly lit by gas lanterns hanging from the ceiling. In one of the rooms, cross-legged monks were locked in a debate about something. From another came deep and continuous chanting, like the chugging of an engine. Between the buildings, I caught glimpses across the darkening valley. Was something out there in the shadows?

The monks kept bowing and signalling for us to follow, and we bowed back and signalled that we were. It was all very friendly, but each time I tried to sneak a look through a window, one of them rushed back and pushed me along. They may have been welcoming, but they had secrets.

They led us into a chamber with cushions on the floor and silk banners on the walls. I think I spotted a hatch in the ceiling, and an old wooden ladder fixed to the roof, but it was tricky to be sure because the room was thick with smoke from incense burners. We coughed as our lungs adjusted from the pure valley air.

One of the monks lit the gas light on the ceiling, while the other gestured for us to take off our rucksacks and sit down. And then, *oh God*. I smelled it before it arrived, stronger even than the incense. Yak butter tea. It came on a tray carried by a monk only a little older than me, with a black buzz cut. He'd perfected his monk smile, and seemed especially pleased to see me and Pan. I guessed he didn't meet many kids up here on the mountain.

"Tenzin," he said.

"Excuse me?" I asked.

"My name Tenzin."

We smiled and told him our names.

"Atlas," he repeated. "Like book of the world."

He poured us cups of tea and hovered close with the pot, grinning and gesturing for us to drink. I remembered how Tibetan hospitality insists your cup is topped up after every sip. In the end I kept raising the cup to my lips and stopping, as if I'd just remembered something. Tenzin got in a bit of a muddle and eventually focused his efforts on the rest of my family.

I think they'd each drunk three cups of Tenzin's tea before another monk came in, bowing with his hands pressed together. This was an old guy, his face with the shape and wrinkles of a walnut, wearing thick-lensed glasses.

"Welcome to our humble home," he said, bowing again. "You are our honoured guests."

"It is our honour to be your guests," Mum replied. "Are you the lama?"

It seemed weird that Mum asked the guy if he was an animal, but later I learned that *lama* meant the head of a monastery. The man nodded, and there were more smiles and bows. Someone somewhere banged a drum.

"Please, what brings you to Yerpa Gompa?" the lama asked.

"We have come as your friends, seeking information."

"However we can help you, we shall. You are our honoured guests."

They went back and forth again over who was the most honoured, until the old monk finally sat opposite us.

Dad looked to Mum, who nodded.

"We wish to see the Drak Terma," Dad said.

The lama's smile faltered, just slightly, at the edge. He noticed that Mum had finished her tea, and waved to Tenzin. Until then Tenzin had been eagle-sharp with the top-ups, but my dad's statement threw him. He rushed to refill the cup, but his smile suddenly seemed forced, and his eyes flicked anxiously between us.

"We have nothing but respect for your traditions," Mum added. "We can only assure you that we would not be here were it not a matter of vital importance."

"May I ask what matter this is?" the lama asked.

Mum told him everything: about us, the emerald tablets, Marjorie and the People of the Snake, the mysterious lost civilization and the clues that seemed to lead to Mount Kailas. It was a lot to take in. I'm not sure I would have believed it, but the old monk listened and nodded, and then sat thinking.

"You have had quite a journey," he said, finally.

"Yes," Dad agreed, "but it is not over yet. The organization we spoke of will not stop until they have destroyed everything. The only way we can stop them is to get to the end first, to save whatever we find from destruction and show the world. We cannot do that without the Drak Terma."

Gaslight reflected off the lama's glasses. "The Drak Terma," he said. "It is said to give a route to a secret in the heart of Mount Kailas. A pathway to the gods."

"We believe that it leads to the information we're after," Pan explained. "A Hall of Records hidden in the mountain."

"So you do not believe in the gods?" the monk asked.

"We respect your beliefs," Mum answered.

"But you do not believe in gods?" he persisted.

Why didn't Mum lie? Why not tell the old guy that we totally believed in his gods, and we were here to protect them? That seemed to be what he wanted to hear. Instead Mum shook her head and sipped her tea.

"We are historians. We respect the history of your faith."

"But you are not religious people?" the lama said. "You do not believe the legends of the gods, or the stories of the Crystal Mountain?"

"No," Dad admitted. "No, we do not."

"But the things you ask are things that can only be given to a holy person."

"We are hoping you will make an exception," Mum said.

The monk smiled again. "I understand. This is something on which I must think very deeply. You may remain here as our guests. I will ask for food to be brought, and more tea."

"You are very kind," Mum replied. "We feel very honoured."

He *was* kind, but all this "honoured" stuff was getting a bit much. We wanted to see the Drak Terma, not to steal it. We'd be in and out of here in ten minutes if he let us have a look. I was about to tell him that, but Tenzin took the chance to fill up my tea even though I'd not had any, and blocked my view. Had he known I was about to argue and deliberately got in the way?

Tenzin followed the lama from the chamber and closed the door on his way out.

"They've locked us in," Pan whispered.

"No," Mum said. "They've closed the door. We're here as guests."

"Something's not right about this place," I insisted. "The monks look shifty. They know something we don't."

"Perhaps," Mum agreed. "If they choose to tell us, then we'll be grateful."

"But what if they don't?" I asked.

"Then we accept that. We made a promise to Takara, remember?"

I remembered, but surely that didn't matter? She wasn't even here. "You mean after everything we've gone through, it all comes down to whether a few mad monks decide whether to let us in on their silly secrets?"

"They're not mad, Jake," Pan said. "And their beliefs aren't silly. We have to respect them."

I didn't really think the monks were mad; I was just frustrated. Until now we'd gone out and got whatever we were after. But we'd stalled here on this mountain, begging for permission to carry on.

"We should get some sleep," Dad suggested, reducing the gas lantern to a dim glow. "This could take a while."

I peered through the window to see where the lama had gone, but Tenzin's head popped up outside, blocking my view again. He held up a football, his grin now impossibly wide.

"You like Manchester United?"

I shook my head – not particularly. Almost everywhere we went locals asked me about football in England.

"Will you play?" he asked.

Now this was interesting; a chance to get out of this room and have a poke around...

"I'm going out," I called.

"No, you are not," Mum replied.

"But that monk wants a kickabout."

Mum saw Tenzin's face in the window, and returned his smile. "Just don't go far, Jake. We need to—"

"I know, I know. We need to show them respect."

Tenzin was waiting for me in an alley between two of the prayer chambers. "Hey, Manchester United," he said.

He showed off some crazy skills: super-fast keepy-uppys, headers and flicks off his shoulders.

He kicked the ball to me, but his smile wobbled when I just shrugged, and he realized that I wasn't really deserving of the nickname he'd given me.

I booted the ball back and gestured for him to give me another display so I could snatch a look around. It was dark now, but gaslight flared through the chamber windows, and shadows flickered around the ledges. Close by, a narrow flight of wooden stairs led higher up the rock face, where I could just about see three monks. Starlight glinted off spectacle lenses, and I realized one of the men was the old lama.

Tenzin kicked the ball back to me to get my attention.

"Manchester United. You be in goal."

Those monks looked dodgy. I needed to see more, but I'm not hugely proud of what I did next. Grinning at Tenzin, I toe-punted the ball as hard as I could so it shot past him and along the alley. I cheered like I'd scored a goal, but Tenzin looked torn – he'd obviously been told to keep an eye on me, but his ball could roll off the mountain if he didn't go after it.

He signalled to me to stay put, and scampered after the ball. "Wait. Manchester United, wait there!"

I slid my smart-goggles on and set them to night vision to watch the monks at the top of the steps. Two of them stood by a line of prayer wheels, listening to the lama as if they were receiving instructions. It seemed strange; surely a monk would know what to do with a prayer wheel? Rather than spinning the things, the monks were turning them slowly, deliberately, like they were setting them to exact positions.

"Manchester United!"

The football thumped into my head, sending me tumbling to the rocks. Tenzin rushed over and helped me up, babbling apologies.

"Sorry, sorry. Accident. Forgiven?"

I smiled and nodded, but I didn't think he'd hit me by accident. He had taken me out, to stop me from seeing what was going on at those prayer wheels.

The monks were keeping secrets. My parents wanted us to be patient, but there was no time. We had to see the Drak Terma soon, to stay ahead of our enemies. If that meant breaking a few rules – and a few promises – then that was how it had to be.

I gave Tenzin back his ball and bowed, thanking him for the game. He looked disappointed that I was going back inside, but my smile was genuine.

At last I had a plan.

16

"The Snake Lady."

She repeated the name over and over as the frost crystals of her breath shimmered under the Paris streetlights. She had heard one of the mercenaries mutter it even as she left the headquarters, and then the others snickering like children.

Jake Atlas had given her that name. He had humiliated her, destroyed her...

No, she needed to forget that.

There was nothing she could do about it now; the boy had won. She should have been glad it was over. Her work had been everything, and it had taken everything. Physically it had ruined her: the constant travelling, time-zone changes that left her wide awake in darkness and half-asleep in the day, grimacing through migraines she couldn't let anyone know about for fear they would take it as a sign of weakness.

Perhaps now she could relax, enjoy a meal without fielding a dozen calls. She could have that thing she sometimes craved as she lay awake at night.

A life.

These thoughts were snowflakes through moonlight compared to the usual hurricane of worries that raged in Marjorie's head. She was smiling, even, as she entered a record shop two blocks from the organization's headquarters in Paris. She had walked past the store every day for a month, but never dared enter. Music had been one of the few pleasures she had allowed herself, but recently even that had been forced aside to make way for her work.

But now, barely half an hour after the council stabbed her in the back, she entered the store seeking a record. *La Bohème*, the opera by Giacomo Puccini that had haunted her for so long. She found it on vinyl, and even exchanged a few pleasantries with the shop owner. Then she carried it back into the frozen Paris night.

La Bohème.

The love song of the seamstress in her Paris garret. Really, she didn't need the record; she heard it so clearly, and so often, in her head. Love, life, laughter. Things she could never allow herself because of her work. Now, maybe, that might change.

For several minutes she stood staring at the city rooftops, at flats just like those she had pictured in her favourite opera. She couldn't see into any; instead

120

she let her mind drift, imagining scenes behind steamed-up windows. Couples relaxing and talking. A dinner party, wine glasses clinking, friends laughing. A family around a TV, spending a night together.

Together.

All of them *together*.

And her, outside in the cold.

The record in her hand felt heavier and heavier.

She realized, right then, that she had never felt so alone.

The Snake Lady.

A cold-blooded reptile, incapable of love.

She stared down at the record – *La bohème* – and then, finally, broke it in half and tossed the pieces into the gutter. What had she been thinking? The music was ridiculous. The work was all she had ever had. But it was not yet finished. There was one job left, and she would see it through no matter what.

She had nothing, because everything had been taken from her.

By a boy.

A boy named Jake Atlas.

Now – and perhaps it would be the last thing she would do – she would find that boy, and she would kill him.

17

"I have meditated long and hard."

The old monk paused and stared at us from behind inch-thick spectacle lenses, as if he might break into an even longer and harder meditation.

The boy monk, Tenzin, topped up my yak butter tea.

"I am afraid," the lama continued, "that we cannot assist you with your request. We built this monastery to protect the Drak Terma. We must remain true to that sacred duty."

I had known this was coming, but I couldn't hold back a frustrated groan. Mum and Dad had insisted we respect the monks' decision, and they actually looked like they did, smiling and nodding as if everything was fine.

Nothing was fine.

We *had* to see that document.

"Maybe you could describe it?" I suggested. "That way you wouldn't have to show us."

The old monk shook his head. "It is not the document that worries me," he explained. "It is your destination."

"Mount Kailas?" Pan asked.

The monk closed his eyes, as if just hearing the mountain's name was an emotional experience.

"To you it is a place on a map," he said. "To us it is a place in the heart. It is the Crystal Mountain, the home of the gods, which must never be entered. We cannot help you do so, no matter how noble your intentions."

Maybe this guy didn't understand. Maybe it was a translation thing.

"We think that something in that mountain," I said, slowly to be clear, "holds the secret to saving millions of lives."

The monk nodded. "As I say, no matter how noble your intentions. We will pray for you, to help you on your quest."

I couldn't help myself, my blood had started to boil. "If you want to help us," I snapped, "let us see the Drak Terma."

"Jake, that's enough."

"But we're trying to help *them* too, Mum. They don't know the Snake Lady, or what she'll do when she gets here. You think she'll sit around drinking tea while someone else decides what she can or can't see? She'll come with soldiers and guns."

"Others have come with soldiers and guns," the lama said, calmly. "We have resisted them."

"These people are not like those others," I said.

"Anyone who comes is welcome," the monk replied. "And they will receive the same reply."

He removed his glasses and cleaned them on his robe. "But there is something of which you should be aware. Mount Kailas is said to be guarded."

"Guarded?" Mum asked. "By the Chinese army?"

"No. By something else. Some say it is a spirit, others say it is a living creature. Legend says the guardian hunts those who seek to defile the Crystal Mountain, and in this land legends are not always just legend."

The monk smiled, tiny eyes watching us from his wrinkled face. "Or perhaps it is all just mumbo jumbo," he added.

I glanced at Mum, who no longer looked so convinced by her mumbo jumbo theory. Her jaw tightened as she looked away, staring into the darkness through the chamber window. Was she thinking about last night, and the mysterious invader in our camp? Any other time I would have asked the lama more, but right then we had more urgent concerns.

"We're not worried about guardian spirits," I said, trying to remain calm. "We're worried about an organization who plan to—"

"You have said," the lama interrupted. "And I have replied."

Bones clicked in his knees as he rose. He looked

back at us, blinking and squinting without his glasses. "You are welcome to stay as long as you wish. But please do not ask about this matter again."

And then he was gone, with Tenzin scuttling behind.

"This is ridiculous," I groaned.

"No, Jake, it is their decision."

"It's a stupid old scroll, Mum. We're not going to steal it, we just want a look. So what do we do now?"

Mum glanced at Dad, who shrugged.

"This could be a test," he suggested.

"What sort of test?" Pan asked.

"We have to demonstrate that we're patient, to show respect. Only then will they trust us and properly consider our request."

"You mean we just wait?" I asked. "For how long?"

"I'm not sure. Perhaps a few weeks."

"*Weeks?*" I seethed. "Are you crazy, Dad? The People of the Snake will be here in *days*. They'll tear this place to the ground to find that scroll."

Mum stared again through the window, out across the valley and the freezing night. "We made a promise to Takara," she said. "Perhaps we can appeal to the monks a different way. They might agree to relocate the terma, to protect it from others that come looking."

"Right." I sat up, warming to the idea. "And when they do, we grab it."

"No," Mum insisted. "We gave our word."

For a couple of hours we did nothing. Tenzin brought more yak butter tea, as well as bowls of soup with dumplings. He kept glancing around the room, as if he expected to uncover some devious plan to steal the Drak Terma, but *really* didn't want to.

When every second counts, sitting around a room doing nothing is the worst. No, actually, sitting around drinking yak butter tea is worse. Mum and Dad may have thought they might be able to appeal to the lama, but the guy's mind was made up. I kept thinking about what I'd seen outside, the monks at those prayer wheels...

The Drak Terma. It was up there somewhere.

Well, if the monks wouldn't show us the document, I'd find it myself. If I could take a photo with my smart-goggles, there wouldn't be much they could do about it. We'd have the information and we could leave them to their prayers.

I waited until I was certain my parents were asleep, and sneaked off.

Outside, gaslight glinted off icicles forming above the chamber door. My cheeks tingled from the cold, and a drip froze on the end of my nose. I pulled my coat tighter and switched my goggles to thermal view, scanning the alley. At least a dozen monks were gathered in a nearby chamber, chanting and banging drums.

I crept down the passage, keeping close to the chamber wall. My breaths were tiny frost clouds, and my heart beat a rhythm with the drum. I saw moonlight glint off the prayer wheels at the top of the stairs, but to reach them I'd have to cross the chamber's open doorway, where I could be spotted.

Move fast, stay silent.

I took a deep breath, held it in, and got ready.

"You're not actually going to go for it, are you?" a voice hissed.

I whirled around, ready to defend myself. Pan stood behind me, grinning while also somehow looking furious.

"Hey," I muttered. "I was just ... you know..."

"Trying to find the Drak Terma?"

There was no point in denying it; she knew me too well. "I don't have a choice, Pan," I whispered.

"Yes, you do."

"OK, but we need it. Otherwise she'll win."

"*She?* You mean Marjorie? Jake, you're obsessed with her."

"I'm not!"

It came out louder than I'd meant, and we waited to see if anyone had heard. Luckily the monks were too busy chanting. Pan had touched a nerve. I knew she was probably right, but this wasn't just about me versus Marjorie. We were trying to stop the People of the Snake from letting millions of people die.

"Look," I whispered, "Mum and Dad don't have to know how I got the information. I won't tell them you knew."

"Are you crazy? I'm coming with you. Someone needs to make sure you don't destroy this whole place."

I wondered if that was her real reason. As much as we squabbled, we looked out for each other on every mission. I don't think Pan would have let me go alone, no matter what.

"We need to get to the prayer wheels at the top of those stairs," I explained.

Pan grabbed my arm and pulled me in the other direction down the alley. "Not that way; come on."

Pan had remembered something I hadn't. She led me into another of the chambers. This room was empty other than a golden statue of a Buddha that sat cross-legged on an altar, surrounded by gas lanterns. Its glaring eyes freaked me out, as if they were angry at us for breaking our promise to Takara and the monks. I was about to turn the statue around, when Pan clambered onto a bench and jumped to grab something in the ceiling. The chambers had hatches in the roofs. She grabbed hold of the ladder, which swung down with its top fixed to the hatch, and then she began to climb.

Sometimes my sister is really cool.

I followed her up the ladder, which seemed almost five hundred years old. The hatch at the top swung open after a shove, and a rush of icy night air swept into the chamber, causing the gaslights to splutter. Pan helped me up onto the roof, where we were about halfway up to the ledge with the prayer wheels. We'd have to climb the rest, maybe twenty metres straight up. Pan knew I wasn't keen on heights...

"Wanna go back?" she suggested.

She sounded hopeful, and I wondered if she had brought me here *expecting* me to turn back. But I pictured the Snake Lady and her smug smile at knowing I was too scared to go on...

I ordered my smart-goggles to switch to night vision.

"Let's go," I said.

The rocks were shrap, but also slippery with frost. My legs started to shake from fear before I'd climbed even a few metres, but there were plenty of cracks in the surface for hand and footholds. Pan hissed at me to hurry up, but I was climbing as fast as my nerves would allow. By the time I reached the ledge, my arms were shaking too. I mumbled something about being cold as I helped Pan up, but she knew it was a lie, and smiled.

Sticking close together, we edged along a shelf in the mountainside, about as wide as a pavement, to a short rope bridge where part of the passage had fallen away. The monks' chambers were directly below us. The rocks shuddered with the volume of their drumming and chanting.

Beyond the bridge we reached the prayer wheels.

"The monks were up to something here," I said. "They were turning these wheels really precisely, into specific positions like they were locking something."

"Or *unlocking* something. Did you see the positions?"

"No, it was too dark."

"There could be thousands of combinations, Jake."

I'd thought about that. Pan had told me that prayer wheels were all about scoring merit points, but there were loads of others around this monastery that the monks could spin. Why climb to this lonely ledge?

I moved along the line of bronze drums, leaning closer to inspect each one. It was the first time I'd noticed their carvings. Some were signs from an ancient language, but there were other symbols too – flowers and shells, and fish with big lips that seemed to be kissing. But not all of the wheels were quite the same.

"Look at these drums, Pan. On most of them the carvings are only worn on one side, the side facing out."

"They're worn by the wind," Pan agreed. "So those wheels never get turned."

"Yeah, but these two drums are different. Look, they're worn all the way round. Only these two are ever turned."

"You mean, to open a secret entrance?"

"Maybe, by setting them into a certain position."

"OK, but what position?"

That was the key question, but I sensed the answer was here if we kept thinking. "What are all these carvings, anyway?" I asked.

Pan turned one of the wheels, examining the markings. "It's Sanskrit," she said. "The letters are a prayer mantra. *Om Mani Padme Hum*. It means "Hail to the jewel in the lotus". It's what Buddhists repeat when they pray, to open a path to heaven."

"Or a secret entrance?" I muttered. "What about these other symbols?"

"Those are the eight *ashtamangala*, lucky symbols that represent parts of the body. This conch shell stands for teeth, these fish are eyes..."

"Is there one for the heart?" I interrupted.

"Yes, this one here."

Pan turned the wheel to the symbol. It looked like one of Mum's phone doodles, a little grid of criss-crossing lines.

"This is the never-ending knot," Pan told me. "The heart."

My breath misted the symbol as I leaned close to see. "Pan, do you remember what that old lama said about Mount Kailas?"

Pan thought for a moment, then grabbed my arm. "Jake! He said it was a place in the heart!"

It had seemed a weird thing to say at the time, but maybe it made more sense now. I rushed to one of the two wheels that the monks had turned and positioned it so the heart symbol was facing inward, and then did the same to the other one.

"OK," I said. "You take one, I'll take the other. We'll turn them at the same time, until the heart faces out."

"Turn them anticlockwise," Pan added.

"Why?"

"Buddhists always turn them clockwise," she explained. "If these open something, the monks wouldn't want anyone stumbling on the secret by spinning the wheels. But no one would spin them anticlockwise."

"Good thinking," I agreed. "OK: three, two, one..."

We turned the wheels and stepped back, looking along the ledge and then around the mountainside. I'd hoped a door might open, or *something*. We tried again, this time turning them clockwise, and then again rotating them slower and then faster. But nothing happened.

Icy wind rattled the prayer wheels, but otherwise – silence.

"The monks have finished praying," Pan said. "If they spot us up here they'll kick us out. Then we really will have no chance of seeing the terma."

She was right, but this had been my only plan. Was it really over? Six months of treasure hunting and it all ended on this freezing mountain ledge? I cursed and slapped one of the prayer wheels so it spun again.

"Come on," I said. "Let's get back."

As we moved for the rope bridge, its wooden

planks began to tremble. I looked up, fearing an avalanche, but all I saw was stillness and stars.

"Jake..." Pan breathed.

I followed her gaze back to the prayer wheels. A section of the drum line, just four wheels, had risen like a tollgate, revealing an entrance into the mountain. It was just a crack in the cliff, half the height of a door, but it was a crack that the monks had gone to a lot of trouble to hide...

18

"How dangerous can this really be?" I whispered.

That was a dumb thing to say, but I meant it at the time. We'd been in secret caves before, but ones carved by ancient civilizations whose hobbies included ripping out your heart while you were still alive. This one was carved – or guarded at least – by Buddhist monks, who weren't famous for their blood-thirstiness. What was the worst that could happen?

Like I say, I wish I'd paused to think about that.

"Stay close," Pan hissed.

I was already so close that I could feel my sister shaking as we edged deeper into the curving dark-ness. The passage into the mountain was so narrow that we'd had to shuffle in sideways, and even as it widened, my shoulders still brushed against cold rock on either side. Our goggles were set to night vision, so we saw each other's breath as green ghosts. Beetles as big as mice scuttled into cracks. Above, bats stretched their wings as they settled down to sleep. The ground was squelchy with their poo.

I began to worry that this was just an ordinary cave, but as the passage opened further, the walls changed. Gruesome carvings leered at us from the rock. They were like scenes from a horror film – people impaled on spikes or being burned alive by devils, all painted in garish primary colours.

"What are these?" I asked.

Pan stroked the carvings, fascinated. "They're self-manifested images."

"What does that mean?"

"Buddhists believe that images of gods form by themselves."

"But... They don't actually, right? Someone must have carved them. I bet it was that crafty lama."

"He's not crafty, Jake."

"He's shifty, Pan. He's hiding the Drak Terma. What gods are these, anyway?"

"I think they're protector deities," Pan muttered.

"Well, what are they protecting?"

I felt a familiar tingle in my belly as I edged further along the passage, a sense that we were close to a discovery. Pan, though, sounded more worried than ever, as if the carvings had spooked her more than she was letting on.

"So you don't think the lama was telling the truth?" she asked.

"About what?"

"The guardian spirit of Mount Kailas."

I'd known what she meant, I'd just been trying not to think about it. There was an open hunt against us, and the People of the Snake would be coming to Tibet soon. We had enough to worry about without adding monsters.

"Nah," I said. "He just made that up to scare us off. If there's some guardian monster out to get anyone who wants to climb Kailas, why's it not here now? We're trying to steal the Drak Terma after all, and that's—"

"Jake, watch out!"

Pan grabbed my arm and yanked me back from a long drop into darkness. We'd reached the end of the passage, where a moat-like chasm guarded the core of the mountain. A rope bridge crossed to another ledge, somewhere beyond which gaslights flickered. The bridge was about fifty metres long and totally decrepit. Its planks were rotten, and in the middle it sagged heavily down into darkness.

Pan peered into the abyss, and then shuffled back. "That's deep. You go first."

I cursed, but I could hardly complain; this was my plan, after all. I breathed in, calming my nerves as I took my first step onto the bridge. The rotten plank creaked with a noise like a wailing ghost. The wood was old and damp, but it took my weight. I gripped the rope rails tighter, and edged slowly across the bridge. The wooden planks groaned even louder.

Then, another sound.

A hiss, like a valve being released, echoed around the darkness. Warm air rushed from below, prickling my skin, and the whole bridge began to shake.

"Jake?" Pan called. "What's going on?"

Between the planks, I saw light flicker at the bottom of the chasm. "Looks like a flame," I said. "Maybe someone's down there."

"Someone making a hissing noise?"

"It sounds more like gas."

"Gas? Jake, this valley sits on a gas reserve. The monks use it for their lights, remember? Maybe we've triggered some sort of trap."

"Maybe, but that fire is all the way down there and we're all the way up—"

Right then a jet of flame blasted out of the side of the chasm. Pan tumbled back, snatching hold of the rope just in time to stop herself from falling. I clung on tighter as another rush of fire shot from the rock wall.

"Jake, the bridge is on fire!"

"I know, Pan! What happened to Buddhists being harmless?"

I helped her up and we scrambled for the end of the bridge as more fire jets streaked from behind us, from in front of us, from either side. The flames below were rising too, filling the chasm. We were only halfway across the bridge – could we make it to the other side?

"Keep moving, Jake!"

One of the planks gave way and I fell through, just managing to grab the ropes to stop myself plummeting into the inferno. Another fire jet rushed above me, right where I'd been standing. Below, the rising flames licked my boots as I hung below the bridge.

"Grab my hand!" Pan cried.

It wasn't easy to climb back up, with dragon-breath blasts of fire shooting from every direction. Half of the bridge was alight – ropes burned and planks fell into the flames. The whole thing was going to collapse. I didn't know if we'd burn to death or if the fall would kill us...

"Pan, run!"

We charged across what was left of the bridge, praying we got lucky. The fire was right beneath us, like a rising sea lashing at a jetty. Another rush of flames blocked our path to the ledge. We were trapped – fire sprayed from every direction. But it was only a few metres to the ledge.

"We have to jump!" I yelled.

"Jump through fire? I'm not a circus animal, Jake!"

"There's no choice! Now, Pan. Come on!"

Against all my instincts, I ran for the flames, slammed a boot on the last plank and jumped. Fire singed my hair and lashed from below. I landed on the ledge and tumbled over, swatting frantically at smoke on my arm. I looked up in time to see Pan burst through the flames. She crashed into me and we rolled over, cursing and gasping as the last pieces of the bridge fell into the moat of fire.

We'd survived, but our escape route was gone. We were trapped in this mountain, with no idea if the thing we were searching for was even here. I remembered what my dad had said, about how the lama may just have been testing us to see if we could be trusted. If that was true, then we'd well and truly failed. I prayed it turned out to be worth it.

19

Fire roared higher around the chasm as my sister and I staggered back along the ledge. I shrieked, swatting more flames on my trousers, and then grabbed Pan and shrieked louder as I whacked her back to put out a fire on her shoulder. The whole time Pan just stayed silent, glaring at me like it was all my fault. It *was* all my fault, but she'd really perfected that glare.

I shrugged apologetically.

"At least it's not so cold now," I said.

"We shouldn't have come here," she replied.

I knew what she meant; she hadn't wanted to break our promise to Takara and go against the monk's wishes. Neither had I, but we hadn't had a choice. We couldn't sit around and hope they eventually decided to show us the Drak Terma. We had to go after it before the Snake Lady and her goons arrived and took control.

"Look, we're here now, anyway," I said, "so we may as well carry on. It must be close."

She muttered something too rude to write, but followed me through another tunnel to a circular chamber in the heart of the mountain. It was a natural cavern, with a huge domed ceiling and a floor covered in scratches, as if it had been slashed by a giant tiger. Gas lamps hissed on the walls, between dozens of alcoves filled with scrolls.

"It's a library," Pan gasped. "Do you think this is where they keep the Drak Terma?"

Maybe, but there were *thousands* of scrolls. "So, which one is it?"

It was a headache to me, but Pan looked delighted. She rushed around the cavern, pulling out scrolls and blowing away dust to see their writing.

"Jake, this is incredible. We'd need months to read all of these."

"We only need to read one, Pan, and we've got minutes."

"Well, we can narrow it down, at least. The document we're looking for is far older than any of these. It pre-dates Buddhism."

"So how does that help? They *all* look old."

"No, most of them can't be more than two thousand years old."

"Why not?"

"Because they're written on paper, Jake. Paper was invented around the year 100 in China, about the

141

same time that Buddhism reached this area. But we think the Drak Terma is much older than that."

"So it must be written on something other than paper," I realized.

I was glad Pan was here with me; I never would have known that. "So what are we looking for?" I asked.

"Maybe it's written on bamboo strips. That's what people used for documents before paper. I'll start looking over here."

I rushed to the other side of the chamber and scanned the alcoves with my smart-goggles' torch. I crouched low, then rose to tiptoes, running the light along piles of ancient documents. The longer I looked, the more frustrated I grew. My curses echoed around the chamber.

After about ten minutes we met in the middle of the room.

"Swap over," Pan said. "One of us may have missed it."

I doubted Pan would have, and I was sure I hadn't. Besides, would the Drak Terma really just be shoved in among all these documents? The old monk had told us that they had built this whole monastery to protect it.

Unless...

I crouched and ran a hand along one of the grooves that covered the rock floor. Something was beginning to occur to me.

"Pan? The monks built this monastery to guard the Drak Terma, right?"

"So?"

"What if he meant it literally?"

"What do you mean?"

I was still trying to work it out. "We assumed he meant they built this place and brought the terma here, right? But what if it was the other way round? This was the only place they *could* build the monastery, because the Drak Terma was *already* here."

My torch beam swept the walls until I spotted a wooden ladder against one of the alcoves. I ran to it and scrambled up, turning so my light beamed down across the floor.

"There!" I cried.

The Drak Terma wasn't a scroll, and it wasn't written on bamboo. It was carved on the cave floor, hundreds of letters scratched across the rock floor.

This cavern *was* the Drak Terma.

"No wonder the monks kept this place secret," Pan said. "It looks like Sanskrit, the ancient Tibetan language. Can you get a photo?"

I blinked three times and my goggles snapped a high-res image of the floor. The writing would probably only make sense to our parents, but I didn't know how we were going to explain how we got it. I just hoped they understood. *They* had kept their word, even if I hadn't.

"We did it, Pan," I breathed. "We got it."

"Yeah, but how are we going to get out of here?"

"You are not getting out," a voice replied.

I turned too quickly, fell down the ladder and thumped to the floor. Rolling over, I watched a small, ragged figure shuffle into my shaky torchlight. Yellow eyes glared and a gold tooth glinted.

"Takara?" Pan gasped. "What are you doing here?"

A smile spread across Takara's filthy face, jagged and sharp, like a crack in the rock. "I think that question is better asked of you," she snarled.

I scrambled up, eyes fixed on the woman. "You know why we're here," I said.

"Did the monks permit you to see this place?"

"I... We haven't stolen anything."

She shuffled closer, glaring at us with those burning yellow eyes. It seemed impossible that someone filled with such rage could be grinning. Her voice rose, echoing around the cavern.

"You gave me your word," she roared, "and you gave them your word. You have broken both, as I told them you would."

I stared, trying to make sense of what she was saying. "You got here before us?" I asked.

"You warned them we were coming," Pan said. "But why? You know how important this is."

"I know what it means to give your word and break it," she spat.

"OK," I conceded. "We're sorry. No one needs to know."

"I knew you would betray me. You are your parents' children, in every respect."

144

"What do you mean?" Pan demanded. "What happened between you and them?"

"So they haven't told you?"

Our silence was her answer. The fire went out in her eyes and her grin spread even wider; whatever she was about to say, she was delighted to be telling us.

"I was their contact in Asia," she began. "I worked for many treasure hunters, providing whatever they needed for their missions. Your parents came here, to Tibet. They had been hired to search for an important artefact for a museum. A golden urn."

"A golden urn?" Pan said. "That was the meaning of the Russian name we used to contact you. *Zolotaya*."

"Yes, *zolotaya*," Takara agreed. "The golden urn is a sacred vessel used to choose the next Dalai Lama, the true leader of Tibet. The museum had information that the Chinese army planned to steal it, so that there would be no more Dalai Lamas. Losing it would crush the Tibetan people. Your parents came to find the urn, to protect it from the army. That was what they believed, anyway. I challenged them on their sources, but they gave me their word and I trusted that."

"But it wasn't true?" I asked.

Takara looked away. For a moment the bitterness in her voice was replaced by something like sadness. "I... I joined them on the mission. We located the urn in a secret chamber in the Jokhang Temple."

"The room we met in?"

"Yes, but when we tried to meet the contact from the museum to hand over the urn, no one was there. That was when we heard the first gunshots."

"Guns? Who was firing?"

"The Chinese army. You see, we had been used. Your parents thought they'd been hired by a museum, when really it was the army tricking them. After we took the urn, the army announced that Tibetan rebels had stolen it to install a new Dalai Lama and overthrow Chinese rule. It was the excuse they needed to round up a dozen freedom fighters and execute them in the streets."

"Execute?"

"They shot them like dogs. One was my sister. Another was my husband."

"No..." Pan gasped.

"Yes," Takara said. Her hands tightened, curling like claws. She gazed at the scratches in the cave floor and her eyes glistened.

"Your parents fled," she continued. "They tried to convince me to come with them, but I could never leave my country. I would never forgive myself, or them. They gave me their word. My foolishness and their lies got my people killed."

"That was why they really stopped treasure hunting," Pan realized. "But it wasn't their fault. They were tricked."

"They gave me *their word*. I knew when you came back that you could not be trusted, none of you. So

I came here to warn the monks. They offered you a chance to show them respect, yet here you are. Once again the Atlas family breaks their word."

"Our parents don't know we're here," Pan insisted. "They told us not to try to find the Drak Terma."

"But still you did. I knew it would end this way. Before I even left for this place I sent word of where you were headed."

A trap door opened in my stomach. I edged forward, trying to stay calm, praying I'd misunderstood. "What do you mean 'sent word'? Takara, what did you do?"

"What I had to, to protect this place."

"You didn't tell the People of the Snake?"

"No, not them. I told a hunter, an old colleague. There is an open hunt on your head, remember."

"You idiot!" Pan seethed. "You don't know how dangerous those people are. You worked with them twenty years ago. They're not the same. You think a nice old hunter is going to come and take us away in handcuffs? Whoever's coming is going to do more damage to this place than we would ever have."

For the first time her smile faltered. "No," she said. "He promised to give half of the reward to the monastery, to help protect this library."

"And you believed him?" Pan snapped. "We have to get out of here before—"

The cavern jolted, as though someone had rammed into it with a bulldozer, and I tumbled to the ground again. Another hit, this time even harder, caused rocks to dislodge from the walls and crash down around us. I scrambled up, covering my head as a third colossal strike shook the cave.

"How did you get in here?" I screamed to Takara.

She stared around the shaking cavern, baffled, terrified.

"You followed us in here," Pan cried. "How?"

"There's a secret route, higher up. But I don't understand. What's happening?"

"Whoever you called," I yelled, "is here."

20

We scrambled after Takara as she led us to a ladder and another bridge higher across the chasm, away from the firetrap. We raced behind her, no longer even thinking about the flames that had almost roasted us alive. The cave shuddered, and rocks plummeted past us, only just missing the bridge. As I reached the other side, a chunk of stone hit the side of my face, knocking off my smart-goggles. I dropped to the ground, tasted blood in my mouth, and my world turned crimson. The rock floor jolted as something slammed into the side of the mountain. It felt as if a tank was firing at the monastery.

I grabbed my goggles as Pan helped me up, and we continued after Takara along the passage. The entrance by the prayer wheels was still open, and we stumbled out onto the mountain ledge. More rocks fell from above, smashing prayer wheels and sending them spinning off down the slope.

"Jake, what's happening?" Pan screamed.

I didn't answer; I had no idea.

We ran across the ledge, trying to make sense of the chaos. *Something* was firing at the mountain from the valley. One of the monastery chambers had been blown to rubble and, as I watched, a falling boulder smashed through the roof of another. Flames lashed out of one of the chambers, where a gas line had ruptured and caught fire. Monks staggered out, dragging an injured monk with them.

I tried to control my panic, to work out what was happening. Blood blurred my eyes, and everything was shaking and darkness and noise. Red lights flashed in the sky and spotlights swept rapid circles across the mountainside, beaming from somewhere in the sky.

"Drones!" I hollered.

"What?" Pan screamed.

"We're being attacked by drones!"

I shielded my eyes as one of the searchlights caught me. The drone flew in closer, rotors buzzing and mechanical legs hanging with vicious grab claws. A bolt of energy – a fizzing blue laser blast – shot from the machine and into the mountainside close to where we cowered, causing an explosion of rock and livid blue sparks.

Even above the blasts from the drone, we heard Mum and Dad calling our names as they searched for us among the chaos. We scrambled down the stairs, and they grabbed us in tight hugs. Mum wiped blood from my face and checked the wound on my head.

"Thank God you're safe," she gasped.

I wasn't sure we *were* safe, but we were alive and so were they.

"Someone's using drones," Pan wheezed.

"I don't understand," Mum said. "How did anyone know we were here?"

"It was Takara," Pan replied. "She sold us out."

"Takara?"

"She's here. We saw her in the caves."

"Caves?" Mum pushed me away, stared at me. "Oh, God... Jake, Pandora, what have you done?"

There was no point in lying. We had to come clean, and pray we could still get out of this.

"I went after the Drak Terma," I admitted. "I made Pan come with me, but Takara caught us. She'd already ratted us out to a hunter."

Mum grabbed my arm so hard I winced. Her eyes glared with an anger that I don't think I'd ever seen before – and I've seen her angry a lot.

"We gave these monks our word, Jake! We've betrayed them and led our enemies right here."

"We can make up for it," I insisted. "We can stop this."

I pulled away and ran along the ledge, yelling at someone I'd just spotted fleeing one of the chambers.

"Tenzin!" I cried. "Tenzin, it's me! Manchester United!"

He saw me and waved for me to follow. Maybe the monks had somewhere safe to hide, but this was their home and it was going to get destroyed. I ran after him, gesturing wildly.

"Tenzin!" I shouted. "They're drones. Flying machines. See, with the lights. We have to stop them. Get the other monks. Gather rocks. Do you understand?"

He seemed to, which was impressive considering how crazy I must have looked, with my wild eyes glaring from a mask of blood and dust.

He shouted to some of the monks, who were whacking a fire with their robes. One of them, the old lama who had refused to show us the terma, saw me. His glasses were cracked and covered in dirt. He wiped the broken lenses on his robe.

"This is your fault," he said.

"No," I told him. "Remember we told you someone would come? They're here now."

"No," he repeated. "This is *you*."

I knew what he meant, and he was right. We'd broken our promise, just as Takara had told him we would. He didn't look angry – if anything I'd say he looked sad. But we still had a chance at saving what was left of his home.

I'd had some experience of drones. We'd been rescued by one from a tomb in Egypt, and – in a strange act of madness – I'd ridden one up a mountain in Honduras. Considering the destruction they could dish out, they were pretty fragile machines.

"Rocks," I said. "Get everyone to gather rocks. If we throw them at the drones, maybe we can take them out."

The lama understood, but shook his head. "No," he insisted. "We do not fight."

"It's not fighting. It's saving your home."

"Our home is already destroyed because of you. Now I must protect my people. There is a way out, through a tunnel. You may come."

He turned and called to the other monks, who were putting out fires or helping their injured brothers. They began to follow their leader along one of the paths towards whatever escape tunnel they had prepared.

I was about to yell to my family when one of the drones rushed close to the mountainside, buzzing like a giant hornet. Its searchlights swept the destruction and a voice boomed from its speaker.

"Give up the Atlas family!"

Mum charged into one of the chambers, then reappeared on its roof, having scrambled up through the hatch in the ceiling. She waved her arms, deliberately attracting the attention of the machine's camera.

"Stop this!" she screamed. "We'll surrender. John and I will come down to you."

The drone buzzed closer, its searchlight catching Mum in a savage spotlight. Cameras swivelled as whoever was operating it got a better look at the target.

"There is an open hunt on the Atlas family!" the voice bellowed. "Dead or alive."

"We know!" Mum roared. "Stop this and John and I will come to you. No tricks."

"I want *all* of the Atlas family."

"That's not going to happen."

"Like I said," the voice replied. "Dead or alive."

Mum screamed some pretty rude stuff at the machine, then dived from the roof as the drone fired again. Dad shielded Pan as laser sparks sprayed across the mountainside. Chunks of stone flew around the ledge, and another of the monastery chambers crumbled to rubble.

"Over here!" I screamed. "The monks know a way out!"

They heard me and ran, leaping over the remains of another chamber as the drone buzzed after us, searchlight scanning the rocks. Another laser blast hit the mountain higher up. More rocks fell, crashing into the remaining chambers and tumbling down the slope.

"Where did the monks go?" Mum demanded.

"There!" I called. "Up there!"

We could just see a line of shadows scrambling along a ledge higher up the mountain. We could still catch up if we moved fast.

"Let's go!" Dad roared.

My mum and sister set off after him as more laser blasts shattered rocks. I was about to go too, when something caught my eye in the flashes of light – a glimpse of something back along the ledge. Was it ... a monk?

My family hadn't noticed I wasn't following them, and they wouldn't stop to check. If I didn't go now I doubted I could catch up. But this whole mountain might collapse. I couldn't leave someone behind.

Cursing, I ran in the other direction, dodging another blast from a drone. The machine had spotted me, and its searchlight glared from ten metres out into the valley.

I scrambled to the monk over fallen rubble. It was Tenzin! Blood gushed from a cut on the side of his head, glistening in the drone's searchlight. He looked dazed and confused as I wrapped an arm around him and lifted him up.

"We have to move!" I screamed.

It was impossible; his body was limp. His legs trailed behind him as I tried to drag him back the way I'd come. My family would return as soon as they realized I was missing, but could I wait that long? Around us, rocks cascaded down the hillside, dislodging others and smashing into the chambers.

"Tenzin!" I yelled. "Is there another way out?"

His eyes rolled. He was no help now. What about the cave I'd been in, the Drak Terma library? Maybe we could hide from the drones in there. Only, where was the entrance? I had to find it, then come back for Tenzin.

I lay him under an overhang, where I hoped he'd be safe from falling rocks, and tried to make him understand.

"I will be back, OK? I'm not leaving you here."

His eyes focused on me just for a second, before his head lolled. There was no time to explain any more. I set off, leaping over rubble and scrambling up what remained of the wooden steps.

"No..." I groaned.

The way in was sealed with fallen rocks. I tried to pull them away but they were too heavy, and my arms were too weak. The searchlight beamed at my back. I turned and screamed at the drone – curses, threats, and pathetic pleas – to leave us alone.

To my amazement, it did. The machine rose, and its light scanned the mountainside higher up. I thought that it had gone to hunt for the rest of my family.

Then it began to shoot.

Laser bolts slammed into the slope – maybe a dozen at close range, causing explosions and more rocks to fall. I crouched, covering my head, crying out for it to stop, and then screaming louder as I realized what was happening. The drone wasn't hunting for anyone.

It was deliberately firing at the mountain.

It was causing an avalanche.

The ledge shook like an earthquake. I grabbed a slab of rock, hoping it might anchor me to the mountain, but another falling chunk struck me ... the side and I tumbled over the ledge. I remember rolling, sliding. I remember the flashing, fizzing lights of the drone's laser. I remember the thunder of falling rocks as part of the mountainside collapsed, destroying what was left of Yerpa Gompa and carrying me with it. I remember thinking about Tenzin and my family, and praying they were safe. And then I don't remember much at all.

21

She had always hated travelling, even though she did so much of it. First class and private jets, none of the luxuries afforded to her by her position had really helped. Even the organization weren't powerful enough to alter international time zones to spare her the excruciating jet lag migraines.

They had, certainly, made travel more comfortable. But now the luxuries were gone. Travelling in such style would only draw attention, so she was forced to join the rabble. That was all the boy's fault too. Marjorie made a mental note to remind him of that before she had her revenge.

The train jolted as they approached the end of an appalling sixteen-hour journey from China. Already she felt the effects of the high altitude. As she stepped out onto the platform at Lhasa station, her breath came in feeble rasps and wheezes.

She clicked her fingers, beckoning a porter who scuttled over with a canister of oxygen. She snatched it from him, strapped its plastic mask over her mouth and breathed.

Better.

She needed to stay strong, focused.

At the security check, she handed a sour-faced officer one of her fake passports. She had taken a gamble that Lord Osthwait had been too busy to cancel them, or her credit cards. She had used both to secure a berth on the train, and then again to check into the only decent-sounding hotel in Lhasa, the Shangri-La.

The hotel was a disappointment; Marjorie had no idea how the place had been awarded *one* star, let alone five. She spotted a cobweb in reception, and the view from her balcony was underwhelming, to say the least. Lhasa was a dreary cluster of box-like buildings with little architectural merit, and the Potala Palace didn't impress Marjorie at all. She prayed she wouldn't have to spend long in this city. She would rest, and tomorrow she would seek the information she needed to locate the boy.

She fell asleep thinking of how she would end his life.

22

I woke in darkness. Not a sliver of light.

My body was twisted up like one of Mum's yoga positions. One arm was trapped behind my back, the other crammed between boulders above my head. My right knee was touching my chest, and my left leg was buried under rocks at a ninety-degree angle to my side. Above me were more and more rocks.

I was alive; that was something. But I was *buried* alive and alone in the dark and I couldn't move, so I didn't really see the bright side of things. I tried to scream, but all that came was a dry retch. My mouth was full of grit and earth. I spat some out and my breaths came faster as my mind registered the horror of my situation. I finally managed a scream, and then another, as one of my arms twisted tighter, agony bolting up my shoulder. I tried to fight the panic, but it hit me like another avalanche, and for several minutes I just screamed, until my voice ran dry and I lay gasping in my mountain tomb.

I closed my eyes, praying that when I opened them again I'd be back in the monastery chamber, with my family. My dad would be snoring, music would be blaring from my sister's headphones, and my mum would be awake, keeping watch, keeping me safe.

I opened my eyes to see only darkness.

I tried to calm my mind, tried the breathing thing Mum had taught me, hoping some clever plan might appear in my head. But nothing came – no way out. How could I escape if I couldn't move? I cried out again and then lay still, my screams bouncing around the rocks. Then, silence.

No, wait.

There was another sound. A grunt, and a snort, like a dog. Was someone up there, on top of the rocks? I tried to yell, but the words caught in my throat. Panic was replaced by relief, then by panic again that whoever it was might walk past.

I heard it again, louder this time, closer. The *thwap, thwap* of bare feet on stone, and the clatter of a tumbling rock.

"Help..." I rasped. "Down here..."

I was about to call out again, when the feet stopped. I heard another grunt. And then deep sniffing, like a creature on a scent.

I held my breath.

That noise. It wasn't human. Even buried beneath

the rocks, covered in dirt, with my ears ringing with my own screams, I just *knew*. Whatever was above me wasn't a monk or my family or a hunter. It wasn't a person.

But it was looking for me. I can't explain the terror I felt, a fear that had nothing to do with being buried alive. Right then I didn't *want* to be saved, not by whatever was up there. I felt safer in the darkness, hidden under the rocks.

The creature began to move again, faster now over the rocks, as if it had been spooked. I lay still, my breath still held even as my lungs begged me to let it go.

For several seconds, I heard nothing other than the frantic beating of my own heart. Finally, I let my breath go in a gasp. Then I heard another noise. More scrabbling, more rocks tumbling. Was it coming back?

God, please, no. Please, just go away.

"Man... ted..."

But... That definitely sounded human. Broken bits of words, cries half-drowned by stone. I heard feet scuffing around the surface, the clatter of rocks being pulled away.

"Manchester United!"

"Tenzin!" I croaked. "Tenzin, I'm down here!"

"Manchester United!"

Spears of moonlight pierced the gaps, stinging my eyes after so long in the dark. Squinting, I glimpsed

162

the boy monk in silhouette, frantically heaving at rocks as he battled to reach me.

"Manchester United. I am coming."

I must have gasped a hundred thank yous as he freed my limbs, and then a hundred as he helped me out. I knew I looked a total mess: my eyes red and streaked with tears, my lip swollen and nose bleeding. Tears in my shirt and trousers revealed cuts all over me, but still Tenzin grinned as he lifted me up.

I wrapped him in a feeble hug – partly for the support, but also out of pure gratitude. "Thank you, Tenzin," I groaned.

He'd torn some of his robe to make a bandage for his head, but blood from the cut had seeped through and oozed down his cheek. He wasn't smiling any more – his face was lit with sweat, and his toothy grin had been replaced by something more like confusion, or fear. His eyebrows were sunken and the lines of a much older person creased his forehead.

"You saved me also, Manchester United."

I knew what he meant; I'd gone back to rescue him on the ledge. But that had just been instinct; anyone would have done that. Tenzin had come looking for me.

I hugged him again, and I think I might have cried. I was embarrassing him now, so I sat on the rocks and gazed around the remains of Yerpa Gompa: shattered chamber walls, fragments of banners, and bronze Buddha statues bent and twisted by the rockfall.

"The monks," Tenzin explained, "they go."

He pointed upwards, and I guessed he meant somewhere over the mountain. "Your family," he said. "They with the monks."

I was relieved, but the more I thought about it, the less it made sense. Why hadn't they come back to find me? Tenzin had seen them *escaping*, but did he see them *escape*? The only reason my family wouldn't come back would be because they *couldn't* come back. They couldn't have been killed; they'd been too high up the mountain to be buried in the avalanche. But ... had my family been caught?

23

We scrabbled around the mountainside until the sun began to rise over the valley. We hauled rocks, called out names, and shone my smart-goggles' torch between gaps, making sure no one else was trapped in the avalanche. Tenzin kept insisting that everyone escaped, but I had to be sure.

Exhausted, we sat watching morning tease its way over the ridges. A Himalayan vulture swept silent circles over our heads.

We'd been working so hard that I hadn't felt the chill. Now it stung my fingers and crept up my arms, which began to shake. Maybe it was shock too, but soon my whole body was shuddering.

Tenzin didn't seem to notice the cold at all. He'd gone silent since we stopped searching for survivors, and sat staring across the debris of the avalanche. He kept shifting so I couldn't see his face, and wiping his eyes and nose with torn ends of his robe. I found a flask of water amid the rubble and offered him some, but he shook his head and turned away.

"What's up?" I asked.

He looked at me, his eyes watering as he struggled to find an answer.

"*What's up?*" he said, finally. "Many monks spend whole lives here at Yerpa Gompa. It is big tragedy."

Oh! He was upset about *that*. But no one had died, and they were just small buildings. "Can't you join another monastery?" I asked.

"They are not this one. I feel like my heart is gone."

That seemed over the top, but he was obviously upset, so I didn't reply. His eyes rippled, dawn reflecting in tears as he stared across the valley.

"Why did you do this?" he said.

"It wasn't me, Tenzin. It was one of the hunters."

I felt bad for him, but I needed to focus on my family. I had to assume they'd been caught. That meant I had to reach Mount Kailas more than ever. If I could find the Hall of Records, if that's where the Drak Terma led, I could use it as a bargaining chip to free my parents and sister. Without it, I had nothing. There was no time to rest or worry about the cold. I had to get to the Crystal Mountain, even if it meant hobbling there on battered legs.

I grabbed a blanket from the ruins, tied it into a sack and stuffed it with whatever seemed useful – a shawl, a broken lantern, a woollen hat.

"We need equipment," I muttered. "Tenzin, did you have a satellite radio, GPS positioning or anything like that?"

He stared at me, baffled, then picked something up from the rubble.

"Yak butter candle?"

I smiled, realizing I was being silly. Of course the monks didn't have that high-tech kit. I was so keen to get moving, I wasn't thinking properly.

"Tenzin, I need your help."

"Yes. I will guide you back to Lhasa."

"No, not Lhasa. I have to reach Mount Kailas."

Something like a smile creased the corners of his mouth, but he didn't look happy. He gazed back to the valley as the wide-winged griffon continued its slow sweep across the dawn.

"No, Manchester United. It is against my religion to help you enter that mountain. And you cannot without the Drak Terma."

Should I tell him that I had found the Drak Terma and photographed it? Those Sanskrit words carved on the cave floor... Reaching Kailas was pointless unless someone could translate them for me so I knew where to look for the Hall of Records. I was fairly sure Tenzin could read it, but then he'd know I had broken my promise to his lama, and he'd *never* help me. I had to find someone else to read the terma.

It looked like I was going by myself. I'd never felt so determined to reach any place in my life, or less prepared for the journey. The GPS on my smart-goggles was broken, and I'd need to find food, transport, new clothes. No one knew I was heading to Kailas, and only I had the Drak Terma, but the mountains would be swarming with bounty hunters looking for me. And was something else out there too? I'd tried not to think about it, to focus on the real problems, but I couldn't forget the sound of bare feet over rock, the grunts and the sniffs, and the ice-cold terror of knowing that whatever it was, it was looking for me...

Even my mum had looked uncertain when the lama warned us of the guardian of Mount Kailas. Maybe it was just a story, maybe not, but it didn't really make a difference. My family might be in danger, so I had to reach Kailas no matter how many monsters, hunters or mercenaries were in the way.

I was about to set off, when Tenzin jumped up and marched off down the mountain.

"Where are you going?" I called.

"To Kailas," he replied.

I scrambled after him, stumbling in my rush to catch up. Was he going to help me after all?

"That's amazing. Thank you, Tenzin."

He kept walking, springing from rock to rock like a goat.

"No," he called. "I go alone."

"But... What?"

"There is something important there for me also."

"You mean on the mountain?"

"No. No one climbs the Crystal Mountain. The thing I seek is close to it, at the bottom."

"Wait! Tenzin, just stop, will you?"

He did, finally, but when I caught up I was so out of breath I could barely get the words out. "What are you looking for?" I wheezed.

"A chorten."

"Chorten? You mean a memorial marker?"

"Yes. A special chorten that honours the holy man who built this monastery. I must pray at this place for permission to rebuild Yerpa Gompa."

Hang on, this was interesting! Tenzin was going exactly where I needed to go. I could tag along and find someone to read the Drak Terma along the way.

"Wait," I called, catching up again. "You're right, Tenzin. I can't climb Kailas without the Drak Terma, and that's now destroyed under these rocks. So my mission is over. I promised myself that when it ended I would help you rebuild this place, so I'm coming with you."

"No, you are lying."

"I'm not! This was my fault and I want to make up for it. And I have nowhere else to go. I won't survive out here without your help, you know that. You can't leave me to die. I thought monks were all about helping people?"

He stopped, and sighed. "You promise you only come to help?"

I swallowed, and crossed fingers in my mind. "I promise. I know that doesn't sound like much considering what happened, but I'll come with you and I'll help you rebuild the monastery."

"That is only reason you come?"

"The only reason."

"Then come, if you can."

"If I can?"

He set off again, and finally his smile returned. "It is long walk and you have weak legs."

Look, it was just a little lie. I really did want to help Tenzin. I would find his chorten with him and help rebuild his home. But that would have to come after everything else – translating the Drak Terma, using it to find the Hall of Records and saving my family.

A pang of guilt stabbed my insides as I set off after him over the rocks again, but I ignored it. I had nothing to feel bad about; I was doing what I had to do, and that was that.

24

If everything went our way, if the weather was on our side, if we found food and shelter and avoided altitude sickness, dodged police and army checks, and who knew how many professional hunters lurking in the mountains and hoping to claim the reward on my head, it would be a six-day hike to Mount Kailas. So, really, we had no idea how long this journey would take.

At first we walked in silence, sticking to the edges of the valleys to avoid the tough mountain climbs. But eventually each valley closed in and there was no way onwards without going up. For the first five hours Tenzin spoke only in grunts and gestures, warning me of loose rocks. He'd indicated our route with his hands – up and over, up and over, crossing the valleys like a dinghy struggling against waves. It was the fastest and most direct path across the

Tibetan plateau, but also the toughest – a relentless slog from one climb to the next.

From the top of the first pass we saw the mountains we were headed towards: gleaming pinnacles that looked impossibly high. I asked Tenzin which was Kailas, but he still wasn't talking to me, and merely began trudging downhill.

It was tough to keep up. Tenzin lived in these mountains, so his legs were used to climbing, and his lungs to the altitude. He was skinnier than me, but his stamina and strength were incredible. After that first climb I felt like I had nothing left, that I'd struggle to make it even to the next valley.

It wasn't just the steepness of the hills. The altitude meant my body was getting less oxygen, and I ached all over. One of my knees had puffed up, and I wondered if I'd broken a rib, because each time I breathed in, it felt like a gorilla was punching me in the chest.

That first morning of the hike was the hardest thing I'd ever experienced. I'd thought I was fit, but nothing had prepared me for those hills. Halfway to the second pass, both of my legs went rubbery, like they were made from putty, and I collapsed. Tenzin waited while I massaged my thighs to bring them back to life. I guess he saw the worry in my face, because the third time I dropped he trudged back to help. He crouched beside me and gestured for me to stop rubbing my legs.

He stared for a moment at my thighs, and suddenly

punched both of them incredibly hard. I shot up, crying out from shock more than pain, but, amazingly, it worked.

"Was that a special Tibetan technique?" I asked as he helped me stand.

"No."

"Oh. So it was something you were taught?"

"No."

We kept going, up green-grey craggy slopes and across valleys where nothing seemed to live. We walked for an hour, rested for ten minutes, and walked again. I'd not forgotten that we were being hunted, but I just focused on surviving. The valleys were so still that I felt sure we'd spot any danger. Really, treasure hunters could be hiding anywhere. The stillness and silence of this place just made *us* easy to spot.

But I did think I saw *something*. Maybe I was just paranoid, or maybe it was exhaustion, but two or three times, as I scanned the steep valley sides, I swear I saw movement among the rocks – something sinking out of sight. I shoved my smart-goggles on and studied the landscape.

"Do you see something, Manchester United?"

What could I say? If it was a hunter, why hadn't they attacked? If it wasn't, well, that made even less sense. I slid my smart-goggles back into my pocket. "Nothing," I mumbled. "Let's keep going."

We'd been hiking for half a day when we came

across the first proper signs of life – a camp at the edge of a valley. It was just one tent, black and rectangular and supported by guy ropes fixed to wooden stakes. But it looked creepy and military and suspicious.

"Could be the People of the Snake," I whispered.

Tenzin looked at me like I was an idiot. "That is yak wool tent. Tibetan farmer's home."

"Oh. Right."

I didn't want to be seen by anyone, even a farmer, but we needed supplies. I slid on my smart-goggles, set them to *zoom* and studied the camp. I spotted plastic containers with water, strips of meat drying on frames and washing on lines. My mind went into that zone again, seeking opportunities and making plans...

"Right," I said. "We need to steal food, water and clothes. So we'll need a distraction. Tenzin, if you can reach those rocks across the hill and cause them to tumble down to—"

"I just go and ask."

Before I could protest, Tenzin was strolling down to the yak camp.

I watched him approach, terrified that he'd been wrong and this was a hunter in disguise. I was about to yell to him, when one of the farmers emerged from the tent. There were a lot of smiles and back slaps, and some kids came out and hugged Tenzin, and they all sang a little song. The farmer gave him coats and clothes, containers with food and flasks of drink, and Tenzin struggled to carry it all back up the hill.

He plonked it down, and for the first time since his monastery was destroyed, his eyes lit up.

"Now we have supplies."

"Great job!" I replied. "Lucky you knew that farmer."

He looked confused. "I didn't."

We rested by a boulder and tucked into some of the food; chewy yak meat jerky and tsampa bread that was so hard I could have swapped it for one of the rocks and not known the difference. We slurped soup from one of the flasks, passing it back and forth and grinning as it dribbled down our chins. I even downed some yak butter tea. We were careful not to scoff everything – those supplies might have to last a while.

The real score from the farmer, though, was the clothes. I got rid of my torn hiking trousers and top and replaced them with baggy Tibetan pants, a yak-wool shirt and a sheepskin chuba tunic that was heavy but warm. It was a great disguise too. Now I looked like a local.

We stored the rest of the supplies in rug-bundles over our backs and continued on the trek. I won't go on about how hard it was – just take my word that it was. But I was determined to keep moving; I didn't want to waste any time at all. Even so, it didn't seem like we were making any dent in the distance. Each time we summited a pass, Kailas seemed just as far away.

I knew it was my fault – without me Tenzin could

get up and down the valleys at twice the speed – but it didn't help that he stopped so often. He stopped to pray each time we passed a chorten, and paused to chant at every prayer flag. It was so frustrating. I wanted to respect his religion, but did he really have to do it *so much*? The worst was coming across bronze prayer wheels built into a hillside. Those delayed us for *ages* as he marched back and forth, spinning the drums and chanting *Om Mani Padme Hum*. It was infuriating! How many sins could a twelve-year-old monk have committed?

With each exhausting mile I grew more convinced that we needed another way to reach Kailas. We were still a five-day trek away at a good pace – and we were definitely not going at a good pace.

Our chance came late that day as a vicious chill crept along the valley and my breath began to come in frosty clouds. I think it might have been our seventh pass, and it revealed a wide view of the valley below. A road cut across the bottom of the hill, with a three-wheeled truck parked at its side. Two farmers were tossing animal hides from a wooden storehouse into the truck's open-back trailer.

"Yak-hide smugglers," Tenzin muttered disapprovingly. "These men kill yaks for their leather, which gets good price outside Tibet."

"Smuggle?" I sensed an opportunity. "To where?"

"West, to India."

"You mean the direction we need to go?"

"Yes, that way."

"Tenzin, are you ready to run?"

"Run, Manchester United?"

"We need to get in the back of that truck."

"No, Manchester United. These men criminals. It is against my religion."

Everything was against his religion, but we had to get in that vehicle. It was a perfect way to rest, travel and stay hidden.

"I'm going, Tenzin. Are you coming?"

"Please, we can—"

I didn't hear his suggestion; I was already running. My eyes flicked between the smugglers and the ground, I was careful not to dislodge any stones that would warn them of my approach. I stopped around thirty metres away and hid behind a rise of rocks, waiting to make a break for the truck. A few seconds later, Tenzin scrambled beside me. I wanted to reassure him that I'd done stuff like this before, but there was no time. The smugglers tossed the last of the hides into the trailer, and both men climbed into the driver's cab.

"Now!" I hissed.

This time Tenzin came too, his robes snapping behind as he ran full pelt down the hill. He overtook me immediately – seriously, he was *fast* – and leaped into the trailer as it began to drive away. He signalled for me to hurry, but I was going as fast as I could, weighed down by my chuba and slowed by tired legs.

Just as I thought I might not make it, Tenzin reached and grabbed my hand. My boots scrabbled at the back of the truck, and he pulled me up into a pile of yak fur.

We lay together among the hides, gasping and laughing, relieved and scared. We'd only been hiking for one day and already we were near breaking point. At last we had a chance to rest.

25

"Guchi, guchi..."

She walked along the line of dusty-faced beggars, stepping carefully over outstretched calloused hands. The destitute always intrigued her, although she had seen far more pitiful examples in India or Brazil. She often wondered why they didn't steal. Surely it made more sense to break into a house than to hope for handouts? She would have had more respect for them if they did. They needed to survive, and the end justified the means.

That was one thing she had always admired about Jake Atlas. The rest of his family were so concerned about protecting antiquities that it held them back from achieving their goals. Not so Jake. He was gung-ho, focused on the end no matter the cost. He would have made a perfect agent for the organization, and for a time Marjorie had entertained the idea of recruiting him. On occasions she had even wondered if she and Jake might become close. Those times when she felt an almost motherly affection for the boy...

That was then.

That was before he stood over her, gloating. Before he stole her files, made her the joke of the organization. Before he had taken everything.

"Guchi, guchi..."

Marjorie paused to study the latest specimen begging for her coins, checking if it was the person she sought and then barged past the trembling hand. Of course, none of these beggars could steal; most were pilgrims who had spent every penny to reach this city in the hope of washing away their sins. Swiping a purse to pay for food would get them all dirty again. It was pathetic, really.

Marjorie had been searching for hours. There were *so many* of them: crouched beneath prayer wheels in the Barkhor, sprawled on their bellies in front of the Potala, scrabbling outside the Jokhang muttering the same irritating plea: *guchi, guchi*. She could only see their faces by giving them coins, so they looked up to smile. Even then it was tricky to identify features beneath the dirt, and she was running out of change.

She was running out of time, too. Lord Osthwait had declared an open hunt on the Atlas family, with a billion-dollar reward. As much as Marjorie despised the pompous old fool, that had been clever. The family were formidable, but they couldn't outrun that many hunters. Eventually they would be caught, and her opportunity would be lost. There was no chance that Lord Osthwait would allow her time alone with the boy. So she had to find him first.

She had one advantage: she knew them. She had listened to the Atlas family's private conversations, recorded on bugs hidden in their home. She had researched their history, read the children's school reports. She knew that family better than anyone.

She knew about Takara.

If the family had come to Tibet, they would have found Takara. They had no other contacts here. They would have been desperate, possibly aware of the open hunt, and sought help from the only person they knew in this god-awful—

Marjorie stopped.

Ahead, one of the beggars, a scrawny creature half-hidden in a heap of shawls, held out a shaky hand. As the woman leaned forward, something glinted beneath her hood.

Something gold.

Not many Tibetans had a gold tooth.

Takara did.

Marjorie stepped closer. She unclipped the brooch from her coat – the emerald emblem of the organization. Until now she had not been able to bring herself to remove it, but this was the right time.

She placed the brooch in the beggar's palm.

The beggar, who still hadn't looked up, stared at the ornament of the snake eating its own tail. Her hand trembled harder.

Marjorie knew for certain that this was Takara.

She suspected the beggar wouldn't admit it, that it would take some persuading to convince her to give up information on the Atlas family. So what the woman said when she finally spoke came as a total surprise.

"I know where they're going," Takara snarled.

26

Something jolted. I woke surrounded by darkness and animal hair, and panicked for a few seconds, shoving away yak hides until I saw sky and stars, and smelled diesel fumes belching from the back of the truck.

I sat up straighter, fearing at first that Tenzin had guessed why I was really going to Kailas and jumped from the trailer as I slept. But he was still there, sitting at the back of the truck, his legs dangling over the end. He was staring into the night in the direction that we had come – the direction of his home.

I slid closer.

"I'm sorry about your monastery," I said.

"Are you, Manchester United?"

That was a good question. I did regret that Tenzin had lost his home, but they were just buildings, which could be replaced. I shifted even closer, seizing the chance to talk. I might not find anyone else to translate the Drak Terma, so I might need Tenzin's help. I needed us to be on better terms.

"How long did you live at Yerpa Gompa?" I asked.

"Since I was seven," he replied. "Before, I wanted to be a footballer. To play for the Tibet national team."

"Tibet has a football team?"

"They are best in world. My father told me."

I nodded, as if I'd heard the same thing. "Why did you go to the monastery?" I asked.

"My grandfather was a holy man, a lama. My father had not become one and he was ashamed. I have a brother and two sisters. Sisters live with parents, one brother becomes farmer, other brother becomes monk. That is way of things."

"So why you?"

"I was lucky."

"Lucky?"

"It is an honour to serve my religion."

He sounded like he believed that, so I didn't ask any more questions.

"It is honourable also to come with me, Manchester United. To help me on my quest."

Guilt rose up my throat, but I swallowed it back and patted Tenzin awkwardly on the shoulder. "We'll rebuild your home, Tenzin, don't you worry."

"Can you rebuild the smell?"

"It smelled of yak butter."

"No, it smelled of incense, jasmine *and* yak butter, and of wet cloth from robes hung to dry, and fresh

184

tsampa from the kitchen, and the moss that grows on the mountain at the start of spring, that smells of Coca-Cola. Or can you rebuild the feelings, Manchester United? The feel of the wall between the prayer chamber and the living quarters, where there was no light so the monks ran their hands along the rock to guide them, polishing it to a shine? That feeling is home. Can you rebuild the shrines as they were, or write again all the scrolls in the library? You can rebuild a house, but is it your home?"

I don't think he wanted an answer, which was good, because I didn't have one. A shard of guilt stabbed at my chest, but I ignored it. It didn't change what I had to do. The end justifies the means, I reminded myself.

We pulled the hides around us and tried to keep warm. This was a chance to get some rest, and God knows we needed it, but for a while we just sat at the back of the truck, staring into the dark.

Eventually Tenzin went to sleep, curled in the yak hides with a little smile, like he was having the best dream. But I couldn't sleep any more, even though I was exhausted. The truck kept rattling and jolting, and the yak fur was like a hairbrush scratching at my face. But, really, it was thoughts that kept me awake. Thoughts of my family.

If they'd been caught, were they safe? Did they need my help, while I was speeding away from them across Tibet?

I kept reassuring myself that this was the right

plan; I had the Drak Terma, so it was down to me to find the Hall of Records. Then I'd have something to bargain with for my family's safety.

That was what I kept telling myself, anyway. But I knew my motivations weren't so clear-cut. Even there, in the darkness among the hides, I kept seeing her...

Marjorie.

The Snake Lady.

That smug smile on her painted lips.

It had haunted my dreams, become an obsession. I was desperate to beat her to wherever this hunt led. To wipe that smile off her face.

The truck turned sharply as it began a zigzag slog up to another pass. Yak hair bristled at my face, long and wiry, and somehow still stinking of the animals' gross milk. I pushed it away and watched Tenzin, whose sleep-smile had spread even wider. I wondered if he was dreaming of being back in his monastery.

I'd promised to help him. I'd sworn that was the only reason I was here. But he didn't really need my help, did he? He had planned to go alone anyway, and he knew Tibet much better than I did. Maybe I should never have made the promise, but it seemed like the right thing to do at the time. I really would help him if I could, but my mission was more important than his.

Wasn't it?

27

"Manchester United."

Tenzin leaned so close that his lips touched my ear, and he hissed a little louder. "Wake up, Manchester United."

I was already awake, sort of. Sleep had come in bits and pieces, broken by yak hides flopping onto my face, the truck jolting over potholes, and hard braking that sent me tumbling when the drivers met obstacles on the road. It was so dark among the hides that I had no idea how long I'd been drifting in and out of sleep, or if it was even still night.

Tenzin shook me again, and I nodded, showing him I was awake I should have been more alert, but the darkness was disorientating, and it took me several seconds to focus.

The truck stopped. From outside I heard the smugglers' gruff voices. Then another, a man's, and in that instant I was totally awake.

I recognized that voice.

I glared at Tenzin, put a finger to my lips and hoped he understood.

The man spoke again, his voice rough. "Government vehicle inspection. We need to search your truck."

It was Kyle Flutes, the treasure hunter I'd met in Honduras while hunting for an Aztec tomb. I say "met" as if we'd had a cup of tea together. Actually, I'd stolen all his treasure and set a wild jaguar on him.

If Kyle was here, then his wife, Veronika, was too. Just the thought of seeing her again made me want to leap from the truck and run, but my legs were rigid with fear. I moved one of the hides carefully aside to peer through a crack in the side of the trailer and saw a sliver of dawn.

Kyle Flutes was arguing with the drivers. He was tough, but so were the smugglers, and they weren't buying his story about working for the Chinese government. I imagined they'd dodged a few officials in their time, and none looked like this: a grizzled white man with grey stubble, arms like fire logs and scars across his face that looked like he'd been attacked by ... well, by a wild jaguar.

Kyle and his wife had sworn revenge on me, so I'd expected to come across them again some day. I'd always thought I'd be with my family when that happened, rather than trapped in a flimsy three-wheeler truck...

I watched stone-still as the men continued to

argue. Kyle was as thick as a brick, but he seemed to understand that the smugglers wanted to keep their illegal yak hides secret.

"We're not interested in your cargo," he growled. "We're looking for escaped prisoners. If you're hiding them, hand them over."

This didn't faze the smugglers, who had no idea they *were* hiding us. They climbed out of their cab, and then everyone started gesturing and threatening.

I shifted to another crack, struggling to see. Kyle had said "we" – so Veronika must be close. She hated my family even more than her husband. Pan had blasted thousands of bullet ants at her in the jungle, and I suspected she'd been dreaming of revenge ever since. I couldn't see her, but I guessed she was in front of the truck, blocking the road.

From what I *could* see, it looked like we were high up on a mountain. To one side was a steep slope, thick with snow painted red and pink by the rising sun. I guessed there was a rock wall to the other side, so there was even less hope of escape that way.

"Manchester United, what do we do?"

I wasn't sure yet. Kyle and Veronika would have chosen a strategic point for this roadblock, a place too dangerous for us to flee on foot. Around us would be sudden drops, ice walls, ravines...

The arguing stopped.

Kyle had brought out a stun gun, instantly silencing the smugglers. "I know your cargo is precious," he snarled. "I won't damage it. I just want to look."

The smugglers could no longer refuse, and Kyle didn't wait for an answer. A crooked smile spread across his scarred cheeks as he stalked closer to the truck. He didn't know I was in there, but the reward on my head was "dead or alive", and I knew which way he'd rather turn me in.

"Manchester United, he is coming."

Kyle edged closer, boots crunching in the snow. He'd promised the smugglers he'd not damage their cargo; otherwise, I suspected, he'd have opened fire into the hides.

"Are you in there?" he called. "Why don't you come on out before this gets nasty?"

Tenzin moved to obey, but I pulled him deeper into the hides. My heart was going at machine-gun speed. I thought about my family and wished they were here. At times like this we always had one another's backs. Part of me still expected them to appear.

I leaned to Tenzin and whispered, "We have to fight."

"No, Manchester United. I do not fight."

"I know, but we have to."

"No, Manchester United. We talk to this man."

"Tenzin, this man doesn't *do* talking. And he doesn't like me."

"Why not?"

"I ... I destroyed this temple in a jungle, and it kinda fell on him."

"Did you rebuild it?"

"What?"

"The temple?"

"No. That doesn't matter."

"It matters."

"It doesn't right now, Tenzin! We have to get out of this truck."

I cursed under my breath, listening to Kyle's boots crunch even closer. He was wary, moving like a Special Forces soldier stalking a target. There was no way he'd be so cautious if he knew it was just me and a monk in here. Kyle was looking for my whole family.

I closed my eyes, trying to get myself into that zone where I could think past my fear. I breathed in and out slowly, discarding options and possible plans until only one remained. Plans were meant to be my speciality, but I couldn't work out if this was the dumbest idea I'd ever had, or if it was ... well, just *really* dumb. Unfortunately, it was the only idea I had.

Tenzin was right: there was no way out of the truck. But could the truck itself be our escape? The wobbly three-wheeler swayed dangerously on corners, and several gusts of wind had nearly toppled it over. We were on a mountain road, with a steep snow slope to one side...

"Tenzin, we need to jump against this side of the truck."

"I cannot fight."

"Not even a truck?"

"Yes, I can fight a truck."

"Then get ready."

"But why?"

I feared he'd refuse if I told him, and this plan needed both of us, so I just shrugged. "Maybe it'll scare him off."

That was a lie – nothing could scare Kyle off – but Tenzin seemed to believe it. He grinned at me, as if now that we had a plan everything was fine.

"*Now*," I hissed.

We hurled ourselves at the trailer wall. My shoulder slammed against metal, and I couldn't help screaming from the pain as the truck leaned and swayed. I heard the smugglers and Kyle cry out in shock. I rammed my side again and again against the corrugated wall. Tenzin joined in, still thinking this was all just to scare Kyle – even as the truck swayed harder, and Kyle finally opened fire.

The stun blast lit the inside of the truck, causing yak hides to fly up and catch fire. Tenzin shrieked and covered his head, but I kept banging the truck wall. I'd known Kyle would fire, and he'd keep on firing until we stopped moving.

"Tenzin!" I yelled. "Help!"

His survival instinct kicked in, and he thrust himself harder into the wall. Another blast sent more sparks and hides flying, so we were no longer hidden. I snatched a glance to my side and locked eyes with

Kyle Flutes. The hunter's grin spread further; he aimed his weapon directly at me.

And then the truck fell.

It toppled over and slammed onto its side in the snow. Tenzin and I tumbled among the yak hides, but I recovered and dragged him with me to the side of the trailer that leaned off the road like a seesaw. Our weight may not have been enough to tip it, but Kyle – who, like I said, wasn't the brightest spark in the science lab – fired again, and the force of the blast did the job for us.

The truck swung, hit the slope and then began to slide over the thick snow. It must have hit a rock because the whole thing went into a spin, tossing Tenzin and me around like socks in a washing machine. Through flying yak hides I glimpsed the road. Kyle stood there firing stun blasts at us, but there was something else too, something more terrifying.

Veronika.

She had blocked the road with some sort of snowmobile, and now she was coming after us. Snow *tank* would be a better description; an open jeep with crawler tracks. There were no windows, just a rally car roll cage with a mean-looking laser cannon fixed on a hydraulic arm. Veronika sat at joystick controls, grinning and gurning as she steered the machine after us down the slope. She looked like a mad pirate at a ship's wheel, with a patch over one eye and flame-red hair thrashing in the wind.

"Manchester United! They are after us!"

"I know, Tenzin!"

"Who is that lady?"

"No one good!"

We had a fifty-metre head start, speeding down an almost vertical snow slope in a half-ton metal sledge – but still she was catching up. She was screaming, but her cries were lost in the rush of wind and the scraping of the trailer against snow.

"Manchester United!" Tenzin wailed. "Where are we sliding?"

I'd been so focused on escaping that I'd not thought about where we were escaping *to*. I scrambled to the front of the trailer and thumped at a hatch to the driver's cab until it swung open, revealing a sideways view out of the truck's windscreen. What I saw was not good.

I turned, yelling at Tenzin.

"Grab hold of something!"

There was nothing other than yak hides, so we grabbed each other just as the front of the cab smashed into boulders on the mountainside. The entire truck flipped up and over. For a fraction of a second we hung in the air with a dozen yak hides; then the truck slammed back onto the snow and continued its speed-sledge down the mountain.

We were sliding backwards now. My view from the windscreen showed Veronika firing her laser-cannon, shattering rocks, and her crazy, grinning face as her ski tank burst through a cloud of snow.

The truck hit another rock and we spun around again. One hundred metres ahead, snow became sky where part of the mountain had collapsed, forming a ravine. There was a smooth, white rise, like a ski jump, and then ten metres of nothing before the slope continued on the other side. We were headed straight for the drop, with no way to change course.

"We have to get out of here!" I yelled.

"But a devil is chasing us!" Tenzin cried.

He was right; we couldn't just jump out the back. Veronika would be on us in seconds. She was even closer now, screaming so loudly that her frozen breath came out like steam engine blasts.

"Manchester United? Think!"

"I am thinking!"

"Think faster!"

We were fifty metres from the ravine. There was no way the truck would clear the jump, it was far too heavy...

I looked away from the windscreen, breathed deeply and tried to calm my thoughts. I wished my mum was there, and my dad and my sister. With them, it just seemed to work. All I had now were my smart-goggles and a load of yak hides.

Unless...

Of course!

I grabbed Tenzin and dragged him to the back of

the trailer. I snatched a yak pelt and pressed it into his arms.

"Toboggan!" I screamed. "Tenzin, toboggan!"

There was no time to explain; I hoped he could work it out for himself. This truck was too heavy to jump that ravine, but maybe *we* weren't.

Tenzin was about to ask more, but I shoved him out of the back of the van. Then I grabbed another hide and leaped out after him.

I hit the snow in a roll and slid behind the truck. I caught a glimpse of Tenzin, relieved to see he'd sussed out the plan. He lay on his stomach on the yak hide, gunning straight after the truck and for the jump.

That's what I needed to do too, but I was out of control. The yak hide slipped from my grip but I yanked it back to my chest. I kicked and rolled, so I was on my belly on the hide, facing up the slope to where Veronika had stopped her ski tank to watch me slide to my death.

She might have got her wish had I not seen the grin on her face. It made me want to live more than ever, just to annoy her. I yanked harder on the hide, steering after Tenzin. There was no time to turn. I was going to go over the jump feet first, but there wasn't much I could do about that now...

I snatched a glance over my shoulder and saw the truck shoot up the snow slide, plummet over the end and vanish. I heard Tenzin scream as he rushed after it, but I didn't see him go over. I raised my legs so the yak-hide sledge fired me off the jump and into the air. I flew ten metres, screaming the whole way. I glimpsed a ball of flames below as the truck hit the bottom of the ravine, and then I thumped down, inches from the edge of the slope – and kept sliding.

My scream turned into one of relief and then a whooping victory cheer as I glanced back and saw Veronika trapped on the other side of the ravine. She revved her ski tank, but even she was smart enough to know it would never clear the jump. I stopped cheering, suddenly aware that if we ever met again she would skin me alive.

And, anyway, I wasn't out of trouble yet. The slope beyond the ravine steepened until it was almost vertical and was littered with boulders. I dug a boot into the snow, but there was no way to slow down. The best I could manage was a frantic slalom, thrusting my weight from side to side to steer away from the obstacles. Mostly I failed, so I pinballed from one rock to the other, only just keeping hold of the yak hide.

Then it was a straight shoot to the valley floor, and all I could do was cling on to my sledge and scream. Wind and snow lashed at my face. I was going so fast, at such a fierce incline, that the yak hide skipped up from the ground and thumped back down, as if I might suddenly start falling rather than sliding. I guess I closed my eyes, because the next thing I knew I was lying in a heap of snow, looking up at the grinning face of my travelling companion.

I'd made it to the valley. To safety.

Excitement shone in Tenzin's eyes as he helped me up and brushed snow from my chuba. He looked like he'd just come off the best-ever fairground ride.

"So," he asked, "are you enjoying Tibet so far?"

Tibet had been crazy, and we still had a long way to our destination, filled with who knew what dangers. But I couldn't help it – I laughed. Tenzin joined in, and we leaned on each other as relief and elation came out in a fit of manic giggles.

Our laughter stopped as a motor revved higher up the mountain. Kyle and Veronika were still there. I grabbed Tenzin, and we set off running across the valley; away from the hunters, but not, I feared, towards safety.

28

We kept going.

Up and over another mountain, across another valley, up and over again. Each time we climbed higher we found more prayer flags. Seriously, I had no idea where Tibetans got them all from; I wondered if there were shops among the hills – *Prayer Flags R Us*. Some hung like dirty washing between bamboo poles, bleached by the sun. Others were piled in heaps over a cairn or chorten, as if the person doing all the washing had given up and dumped it all on the rocks.

Gradually the landscape changed. Valley floors, which had been dry and craggy, became spongy and boggy, and then a swamp, which we sank into shin-deep with each step. I spotted plants – scrubby little things that Tenzin delighted in naming, as if we were on a nature hike. He even knew which ones we could eat.

"Juniper," he called. "And this one is *zheibamedu*. Good for cough."

I didn't have a cough, but I was hungry enough to gnaw every little root he dug up. We'd lost our supplies when we'd fled Kyle and Veronika, so this was all we had. It wasn't too bad; one tasted like liquorice and another could have been parsnip if I closed my eyes, which I didn't because Tenzin kept trying to make me eat a fat grub worm he'd foraged, and I drew the line at that.

He collected some mushrooms too, and some other bits and bobs that he refused to let me try, insisting they were for later. But what really excited Tenzin was poo. Every time he discovered a fresh pile of yak dung, he squealed like he'd found buried treasure. He made a rucksack out of his robes, with two separate compartments. Into one went steaming fresh yak poo, while the other was filled with dried-out dung that he scraped from rocks. Every time I asked why, he just grinned, but if he expected me to eat any of that stuff, then we were going to have serious words.

We stopped hiking when it got dark and found a cave in a mountainside. It wasn't much shelter and it reeked of damp, but it was better than trying to sleep in the brutal cold that attacked the valley the moment the sun retreated behind the mountains.

Tenzin produced one of his yak dung collections with a "ta da", like a magician revealing an empty top hat. What happened next was actually really cool, despite my disapproving scowls. He made a fire out of the dried yak dung! He'd obviously done it before, because it took him no time – rolling the dried poo into sticks, and then cracking rocks together to create sparks. In seconds the dung sticks were burning. The smoke smelled terrible but I didn't care. I huddled closer to the flames as icy wind swept into our cave.

We ate more roots and leaves, and I imagined they were cheeseburgers, which didn't help because they weren't cheeseburgers. But as Tenzin stared into the fire, his smile fell away and he went quiet again. It was as if he'd seen something in the flames.

Seeing him so sad, and knowing I was partly to blame, stabbed at my chest. "You OK, Tenzin?" I asked.

He looked up suddenly, as if he'd forgotten I was there. "Yes."

"Are you thinking about your monastery?"

"Yes."

"Well, we're going to find that chorten. You can pray there, and get permission to rebuild your home. Everything will be OK."

"Maybe, Manchester United."

"You know my name is Jake."

He nodded vaguely, but still there was no hint of his trademark smile.

"Does Tenzin mean anything?" I asked.

"Yes. It means 'holder of the teachings of the Buddha'."

"Holder? Like they're inside you?"

"Yes, inside. What does Jake mean?"

"I... Actually, I don't think it means anything."

"Oh. Then I prefer Manchester United."

I shrugged – fair enough.

"So, what's the rest of the dung for?" I asked. "The fresh stuff? Please don't say it's breakfast."

His grin returned and his eyes glittered in the firelight. "This is for the cold," he explained.

"The cold?"

"What is the word? *Insulation*."

I stared at him, and then the dung, trying to think of any way that "fresh yak poo" and "insulation" made sense together.

"You mean we spread it on the rocks?" I asked.

"No, Manchester United. Not on the rocks."

I watched in horror as he lifted his robes and smeared the steaming stuff over his legs, and then across his chest and up his neck. If you've never seen yak dung, just imagine doing that with a fresh cowpat and you'll get why I was so grossed out.

Tenzin lay back, wrapping his robes tight again, and using his chuba like a blanket. "Nice and warm all night now," he said. "You do same."

I stared at the dung, and laughed. If that was the way he did things, then fair enough. But there was no way I was smearing myself with yak poo.

About an hour later I began smearing myself with yak poo.

It was *stupidly* cold, even huddled right beside the fire. Shivering became shaking – my teeth actually chattered, like in a cartoon. Finally, muttering and swearing, I dug handfuls of dung, stuffed it down my trousers and rubbed it into my skin. I shoved more up my sleeves and under my top, and lay back by the fire, cursing about how gross it was.

Almost immediately the cold edged away, just a little, like I'd put on thermals. Through the flames I saw Tenzin watching me. His grin was ridiculously wide, even half-asleep.

"Insulation," he whispered.

I woke.

Something wasn't right. I had that feeling again, that tingle.

The darkness was absolute, so I didn't know where to look, or the way to the cave entrance. Suddenly, two eyes glared at me from the ground – glowing and red, the eyes of a demon. I cried out, scrabbled back and then laughed.

You idiot!

It was just cinders in the fire, pulsing as a breeze rustled into the cave. The wind had died down, but it was so cold that the yak dung on my limbs had begun to freeze. As my eyes adjusted to the gloom I saw Tenzin fast asleep with that same faraway smile, as if this wild icebox was the best place he'd ever slept. I rubbed my eyes, struggling to wake.

Maybe nothing was wrong. My nerves were shattered, that was all. I reached for my smart-goggles and the embers pulsed again.

Behind me, something moved past the cave entrance.

I scrambled around, staring. My heart was a boxing glove pounding at my chest. Was someone there?

"Hello?" I croaked.

Nothing. No sound, no movement.

I waited, rigid with fear, watching the darkness beyond the cave. But still I saw nothing.

I curled up again, groggily reminding myself that no one could know where we were, not even the best hunters in the business. Maybe it was the night playing tricks. Except... The invader in our camp, the creature on the rocks, the flitting shapes I'd spotted around the mountains. Could they *all* be tricks of my mind? Or was something else out there, something other than a hunter? The lama had warned us of the guardian of Kailas, which sensed when someone planned to climb the mountain. Surely Mum was right about that, though: it was all just mumbo jumbo.

Wasn't it?

I regretted the yak poo insulation early the next day. It had dried overnight, and began to crumble beneath my clothes, so I spent the first few hours of the hike itching like crazy. I was finally able to wash it off when we came to a stream among some spindly silver birch trees that covered one side of a valley. We drank water too, and Tenzin foraged roots and leaves for breakfast.

I still had that sense that something was following me, but again I forced the thought away. One problem at a time, as Mum always insisted. First I had to deal with my feet.

Trying not to scream, I tugged off my boots and peeled my socks from a mess of blisters. My heel was one *big* blister, red and raw and weeping puss. On the other foot it was hard to count the blisters, which had congealed together across my toes. I did my best to clean them, but it was too painful and I vowed not to remove my boots again.

"We can't keep walking, Tenzin," I grunted. "Is there anywhere we can steal a car?"

"Steal?"

"Borrow."

"Can you drive a car?"

"Can't you?"

"Why should I be able to?"

I shrugged; he just seemed resourceful like that.

"There is a village," he said, "close to here. They will give us help. Food, transport. Without stealing, Manchester United."

"Are you sure we can trust them?"

"Sure."

So on we trudged, following the river along the

valley, as the trees swayed and creaked, and the mountains closed in on either side. We climbed another hill. We hiked another valley. We scrambled to another pass.

From the top we could see down into the next valley, and the village Tenzin had promised. It was just a few whitewashed houses, a dozen yaks grazing on scrub, and a beaten-up jeep – but to me it looked like heaven. There would be food, shelter from the cold at night, and...

I stopped and stared.

I'd been so busy fantasizing about the village that I'd only just noticed something beside me on the pass: a pile of rocks about the size of a dinner table. It looked like an altar. Scattered on its surface were bones. *Lots* of bones. I recognized a rib cage, a spine, and something that looked worryingly like a human skull...

"What is *that*?" I asked.

"Remains," Tenzin said.

"Remains of what?"

"A man."

I stepped back and stumbled on rocks. *"Human* remains? But ... why?"

"This is how we do it, Manchester United. It is called sky burial. Once your soul is gone, your body is just meat. It is taken to a high place for vultures."

"That's gross, Tenzin."

"Why?"

"Because you get eaten by vultures."

"Not *you*. Your body. Once soul is gone, it is animal feed. I must pray here now, so be silent."

"It's getting dark, Tenzin. We really need to get to that village, to see if they can help us."

"They *will* help, and I must pray."

"Maybe you can pray in the morning? Or pray double at the next sacred thing we pass? It's not like you're short of chances around here."

"No, I pray here."

"That's crazy."

My voice was rising. I wasn't angry, just frustrated. *Everything* was sacred here, everything had to be thanked for or prayed to, and it all took so long. We were out in the open, where any hunter might spot us.

I grabbed Tenzin's arm just as he was sitting down to pray by the altar. "We have to go now."

He shook me off, and from the anger that flashed in his eyes, I thought he might shove me. But he took a breath and sat back down by the altar.

"I pray here," he said.

"But why?"

"Because this is my uncle."

"Your... You mean, your *uncle*?"

"Yes, my uncle."

"So ... this is his village?"

"Yes."

I stepped back, my cheeks burning with embarrassment. "I'm sorry. I didn't know..."

I wanted to apologize again, to tell him to take

as long as he needed, but I didn't need to; he would, anyway. I walked a little way down the slope and sat under some bushes. From there I could see down the hill to the village, although it took me about half an hour to realize *what* village this was. Tenzin had been certain that we would find help here, and it wasn't just a coincidence that we had run across the remains of his uncle up on this hill. That village was his uncle's home. But at that moment I realized something else.

This was also, once, Tenzin's home.

29

They recognized Tenzin from a mile away. Two girls, both a couple of years younger than him, charged out of one of the houses, screaming and shouting greetings.

I thought Tenzin would be happy too – he was about almost everything else, after all – but as he smiled and hugged the girls, he looked awkward, out of place. I wondered if he still saw this village as home, or did it just remind him of how far he was from Yerpa Gompa, and how lost that place was to him now?

Neither of the girls noticed as they bundled him to the ground and attacked him with hugs and giggles. I stood back, feeling like I was intruding, but Tenzin called me over. Perhaps it was just Tibetan hospitality, or maybe he wanted to distract attention from himself.

"Manchester United," he said. "Come, meet my sisters."

They looked a bit wary of me, so I nodded and smiled and said a lot of *tashi deleks*. I followed as they dragged Tenzin to one of the houses, where more grinning family members waited.

They were Tenzin's mum and dad, and they were pretty emotional. I sat apart, to give them space, but after they'd spoken for a while Tenzin's dad came over to me. He was a huge guy, with skin like tree bark and hair like Albert Einstein's. He grabbed me up from the rock I was sitting on and gripped my shoulder so hard that I yelped.

"You save Tenzin life," he said.

I looked at Tenzin, who watched from the doorway. I had invaded his home, broken my promise to his lama and destroyed his monastery, but he still introduced me as a hero. The only reply I could think of was the truth.

"No. He saved mine."

The guy's grip grew even tighter. "You are welcome."

He led us into one of the houses, a windowless room with a round hearth and a cauldron hanging on a chain. I tried not to groan when I saw yak butter tea bubbling in the pot and realized it would be inflicted on me in vast quantities. I was hungry and thirsty and desperate for warmth, but the sight and smell of that tea still made me shudder.

There was no escaping it – a mug of the stuff was shoved into my hand before I'd even sat by the fire. One of Tenzin's sisters sat close, gripping a ladle to top up the drink.

I thought Tenzin and his family would have a lot to catch up on, but no one spoke for at least half an hour. I wondered if I should break the silence with some weather chat, but realized after a while that it wasn't awkward silence – it was simply silence. They were happy just being together.

I thought of my own family, and the times we'd sat around a dinner table. Barely a minute passed without some sort of squabble. Things had changed a lot since Pan and I discovered our parents' secret past, and they'd started training us to become hunters. But we were still often at each other's throats and, as I sat with Tenzin and his family, I wondered why.

I missed them. A lot.

I knew they could look after themselves, no matter what danger they might be in. But sitting there in someone else's home made me even more determined to reach Mount Kailas, to find the Hall of Records, and use it to rescue my family.

Then, suddenly, everyone started singing. One of the girls brought out a tambourine, and the other banged a drum. I clapped along with Tenzin and his mum as his dad stood up by the fire and started dancing – a sort of hip wiggle and thrust, and some jerky head movements, like a chicken. One of the sisters threw him a yak hide, which he tossed over his back, and a pair of strap-on horns – like fancy dress, although I think they were real – and he began snorting as the singing and drumming grew louder.

Tenzin leaned close to shout in my ear. "This is yak dance," he explained.

"It's... " I didn't know what to say. "What is it for?"

"To give thanks."

"Thanks for what?"

"Yaks!"

I nodded. *Everything* was sacred in Tibet, but this one I sort of understood. "The yak gives you a lot," I replied. "You ride yaks, eat yak, wear yak fur, drink yak butter tea, use yak butter candles and make yak dung fires."

"Yes, the yak is very useful," Tenzin agreed, shouting above the music. "But that not why they are sacred. The yak is in us here."

He touched his chest, and for a moment I thought he meant the indigestion you get from yak butter tea. He didn't. He meant his heart.

"When something is sacred, Manchester United, you feel it inside you. It is not just useful, it is part of you to love and protect. A monastery is not just a house, it is home. A terma is not just a scroll, it is something more, something in your heart. And a mountain is not just a mountain."

Man, that was sneaky!

"You mean Mount Kailas, right?" I asked.

"Yes, Manchester United. To you it is useful, like yak. To us it is sacred, like yak. We see same thing, but we see different. Do your smarty-goggles have a way of changing that?"

I pulled my smart-goggles from my pocket and considered them as if perhaps they did have that setting.

I understood what he meant, but that didn't change what I had to do. Searching for the Hall of Records in Kailas upset him, but he'd get over it. After everything my family had been through, I couldn't stop just to spare someone's feelings. I couldn't let them down.

"I'm only here to help you," I lied. "I don't have the Drak Terma, so I can't find what I was looking for."

His eyes brightened, and in the firelight I saw his dad reflected in them, doing the jerky yak dance. Tenzin grabbed my arm and yanked me up.

"Come, dance!" he said.

"What? No way!"

"Come on, Manchester United! Feel the yak in your heart!"

I didn't think I had an inner yak, but everyone was now up and at it, dancing around the fire and making yak noises. Maybe all the candle smoke got to my head, but I was enjoying myself. I was amazed that I *could* dance with the blisters on my feet and cramp in my legs, but somehow I found the energy. Maybe you just do when you're having fun?

That night, nestled among blankets by the fire, it took me a while to get to sleep. I lay staring at the embers, watching them throb as draughts crept under the door, and thinking about this mission. I'd grown obsessed with finding the emerald tablets and discovering where they led. With stopping the People of the Snake from hiding their secrets from the world. With wiping the smile off Marjorie's face.

I'd thought that no matter how we did it, it was worth it. A lot of stuff had been damaged along the way. Actually, *damaged* isn't the word. That suggests it could be repaired. Things were destroyed. In almost every place we'd been, we had wrecked more things than we ever found. That hadn't mattered to me; they were just *things*. I'd never realized, or seen, that to some people they're more than just things. They are *everything*.

Mount Kailas was that to more than a billion people. If I climbed it, I'd be breaking a billion hearts. And maybe that wouldn't be the worst of it. I'd *destroyed* a mountain in Honduras, after all. But I couldn't give up now, could I? I was so close. Maybe my family needed me too. Or was I just telling myself that?

All these thoughts pulsed through my head until I fell into a deep and dreamless sleep.

I woke to dazzling light, as if someone was beaming a spotlight at me. I sat up, pushing back blankets and rubbing my eyes and realized that someone *was* beaming a spotlight at me. One of Tenzin's sisters was wearing my smart-goggles and had activated the torch.

"Good glasses," she said.

I smiled, glancing around the room, embarrassed that I'd slept in while everyone else was awake. The door was open and Tenzin's dad was outside, yelling at yaks. Someone had relit the fire and yak butter tea bubbled again in the cauldron.

I couldn't see Tenzin.

I raised a hand, shielding my eyes from the torch-light. "They're called smart-goggles," I told her. "Watch this."

I leaned closer and gave them an instruction: *"Show last photograph."*

Light flickered on the girl's cheeks, as the lenses showed her the photograph I had taken in the library at Yerpa Gompa.

The Drak Terma.

I tried to sound chirpy, like I was just giving a friendly demonstration. "What do you see now? Can you read it?"

She looked for a few seconds and then removed the glasses. Her smile was gone, and I saw a look that had become familiar to me since I'd been in Tibet. Disappointment. Did she know what I was trying to do?

She dropped the goggles onto the blankets, and walked away.

"Not so smart-goggles," she said.

Great, now I'd upset her too.

I groaned, shaking away the last of the night's sleep. My legs had seized up, and I had to rub them before I could stand. Even then, walking was more like hobbling. I winced from the pain of my blisters, which squelched in my socks.

Outside, Tenzin's dad greeted me with a whack on the back.

"You want to help with yaks?" he asked.

I didn't, but could hardly refuse. For the next hour I joined him, shouting at the beasts and waving my arms as we rounded them into a pen. It was hard work, and I didn't see the point of it because he let them out again about two minutes later.

Tenzin's mum brought me a mug of yak butter tea. I thanked her and didn't even think about how gross it was.

Finally, I had to ask. "Where is Tenzin?"

She nodded towards the mountain we had walked down from the previous evening. "With uncle."

She meant he had gone to pray at his uncle's sky burial shrine. I wondered if he was her brother, and how he had died, but they didn't feel like questions I should ask.

"I'm sorry," I said.

She smiled. "Not sorry. His soul now free."

I headed up the mountain with a cup of tea for Tenzin, but stopped a little way down from the shrine, waiting for him to finish praying. I could hear his chanting, like a whisper in the wind, and the flap and snap of prayer flags that had come free of one of the poles. A Himalayan vulture circled overhead. Otherwise, everything was calm.

From where I sat I could see higher mountains beyond the valley, fang-like peaks and gleaming glaciers, stunningly sharp in the high altitude air. I allowed myself a few minutes to soak it all in. That was something I almost never did on missions. We were always in such a rush, racing to follow some clue. There was rarely time to stop and appreciate how incredible the places were.

I hobbled the rest of the way up the slope and sat beside Tenzin near the shrine. I was far less creeped out than the night before. Tenzin was right; if his uncle's soul was free here, then what a place to be.

I gave him his tea, and we sat for a while in silence.

"Your dad and I herded yaks into a pen," I said, finally, "although I'm not sure why."

Tenzin grinned. "Exercise."

"Eh?"

"That his exercise. Yaks have no need for pens. He docs this to stay healthy."

"Oh."

"Are we friends, Manchester United?"

"I ... I guess so."

"Friends help friends. That is why they are friends."

I nodded, although I wasn't sure what he meant. "We need to keep walking, Tenzin."

"Not walking. My father will drive us to Kailas. It is long drive, but we will be hidden and safe."

That was big news to drop on me, but I just nodded and took a sip of the tea that he offered me.

"You like yak butter tea now?" he asked.

"Not really," I replied, because I didn't want to lie. "But I drink it."

30

Marjorie prided herself on how well she controlled her emotions. She worked mostly with men – arrogant council members or thick-headed mercenaries, people ready to pounce on any "weakness" as proof that she shouldn't be in charge.

Hide your emotions, that had been her rule. But, suddenly, she couldn't help it. She had been smiling for almost the entire journey from Lhasa. A three-day smile! She had slept in guest houses, on itchy and uncomfortable beds with dirty sheets that reeked of stale sweat. She hadn't washed, had barely eaten, and was underdressed for the cold by at least three layers. Usually such an experience would trigger migraines. But she felt great.

After Takara had told her where the Atlas family were heading, Marjorie had hired a guide to take her to Mount Kailas, and purchased a knife: a *phurba*, an ornamental Tibetan dagger. It was a tacky tourist souvenir, its handle studded with fake emeralds and a little smiling Buddha. It was cheap and nasty, but sharp enough.

It was the weapon with which she would kill Jake Atlas.

His family would then kill her, she was sure. But that was fine. It was over now. She was on her way to the end.

And she couldn't stop smiling.

31

Only one road went close to Mount Kailas. I sat sandwiched between Tenzin and his dad in the front of their pick-up truck, disguised in as much spare Tibetan clobber as they could rustle up: another woollen chuba, a huge fox-fur hat that slid off my head each time we hit a rut in the road, and enough scarves to wrap an Egyptian mummy. I'd smeared yak dung on my cheeks to hide my features, but really I looked like a western boy with poo on his face.

We drove and hoped. I had other plans, crafty ways to approach the mountain, but Tenzin and his dad weren't hunters. Just taking me this far was a big deal for them; it didn't seem right to ask for more. We knew we might be stopped, and we had a plan for that.

The mountains grew higher and the landscape

changed again. We'd travelled from lunar nothingness to swamps and woods, but now the trees disappeared and the world turned white.

We'd seen snow high in the mountains, but the further west we drove, the more it filled the valleys. Several times we had to get out of the car to shovel it away just so we could keep driving. Higher up, the white slopes turned neon blue, where shattered ice fields plunged between serrated peaks.

We drove through a few scruffy villages, but after six hours the only sign of life was the occasional yak, shrouded in steam from its own breath. The air was even thinner here; I felt the squeeze growing tighter in my chest with each new valley. My nose became blocked, and my mouth grew parched as I struggled to suck in enough oxygen. We were climbing higher, headed into Western Tibet.

Kailas country.

Mostly we drove in silence, but each time we cleared a mountain pass, Tenzin and his dad burst into a chorus of *"La! So so so so!"* and I joined in, even though I had no idea what it meant.

The closer we got to Kailas the happier Tenzin seemed. He was on his way to find his chorten, to begin the process of rebuilding his home. But with each mile my smart-goggles felt heavier in my pocket – the weight of my lie.

The Drak Terma. Soon I would need to know what it said. Could I ask Tenzin? He would know then that

I had broken my promise, and why I was really here...

I stared out the window, watching snow geese fly low over pristine slopes. We passed glacial lakes, impossibly blue and super-sacred, judging from Tenzin's chanting. We stopped several times to spin prayer wheels by the roadside, gleaming bronze treasures in a world of white. At first there were just a few here and there, but after another few hours they were everywhere. More and more chortens decorated the landscape too. Their golden peaks shone like halos in the late afternoon light.

We kept driving west, with the sinking sun directly ahead. Tenzin's dad slid sunglasses on, and kept glancing at me over the rims. Finally, after a silence that lasted several valleys, he spoke.

"You know why Kailas is sacred?" he asked.

I still wasn't certain, but had a rough idea. "You believe it is the home of gods."

"Not just me. Not just Buddhists. Many people, many religions. To Buddhists it is Kang Rinpoche, the Precious One of Snow. It is the home of Khorlo Demchog and Dorje Phagmo. To Hindus it is Mount Meru, the home of the great goddess Shiva, the centre of the universe. The Jains call the mountain Astapada. It is where their prophet, Rishaba, became enlightened. To the Bon, the mountain is called Tise, the seat of the sky goddess Sipaimen. For some it hides the entrance to Shambala, the land of gods."

"Sounds like a busy place," I said.

He peered at me again. "It is sacred place," he replied. "And dangerous one. The Crystal Mountain is protected. It has a guardian, a spirit that attacks those who seek to climb its slopes."

"It has followed us, Father," Tenzin muttered.

I shot Tenzin a look. Had he sensed it too, or seen it? If he had, why hadn't he said anything? Perhaps he read the questions in my eyes, because he smiled and nudged my shoulder.

"We are safe, because we are only on a mission to find the chorten at the mountain's base. And, anyway, you do not believe in spirits and gods."

Tenzin's dad asked, "What *do* you believe in, Jake?"

I believed that Mount Kailas was the end of my hunt, and that was all. The mountain was bursting with myths and gods and ancient legends, and it was named on the emerald tablets. Surely this was the X that marked the spot – the place the tablets were guiding us to, the Hall of Records.

"Manchester United, it is time."

Tenzin's dad stopped the car. Fifty metres ahead the road was blocked by army jeeps and soldiers in fur-trimmed coats. It wasn't dark yet, but the jeeps had their headlights on, so the soldiers were in silhouette, waving us forward for an inspection. They looked like Chinese military, which wasn't great, but also not unusual. Army inspections were common in

Tibet. Even so, they might have been working for the People of the Snake.

This was where our road trip ended.

"Are we close to Kailas?" I asked.

"Very close," Tenzin said. "Next valley."

"Then we'll go on foot from here."

One of the soldiers trudged closer, fingers tight around his rifle. Even from fifty metres I saw the mist of his breath grow faster. The guy was nervous, which is not good for a man with a gun.

Tenzin grabbed a rucksack from under the seat, filled with clothes and food. He spoke to his dad in Tibetan and they reached across me to touch forehead to forehead.

The soldier was shouting now, beckoning us to drive to the checkpoint. I coughed a few times and shifted in my seat, hoping to break up the goodbye, but Tenzin and his dad kept talking and forehead-touching. The longer it went on, the more I realized how much the monastery had meant to them. It broke their hearts to be parted, yet still Tenzin went away – it was that important. Yerpa Gompa. The monastery I had destroyed, and which I claimed I was here to help rebuild. Sitting there then, I didn't feel like their friend...

Let's not do this. Let's find the chorten and rebuild the monastery. Let's find another way to stop the People of the Snake.

The words were right on my lips, but the soldier

barked at us again and Tenzin and his dad broke up their farewell. Tenzin's dad grabbed a bottle from the dashboard and climbed out of the truck. He yelled to the soldier that the truck had broken down, and lifted the boot to check the engine. With his back to the guard, he poured water on the engine's hot pipes so that a plume of steam billowed up and across the street.

Tenzin threw open the door and we leaped out, hidden by the steam as we darted behind rocks by the road. We waited, checking the coast was clear. The soldier had joined Tenzin's dad, leaning over the engine as they argued about what was wrong.

"Now," I whispered.

We raced over the rocks and uphill through the snow. We didn't look back; we just prayed we would make it to the top. We finally stopped beneath a mesh of prayer flags at the pass, wheezing from the high-altitude sprint.

"Did they see us?" Tenzin spluttered.

"I don't think so. I—"

It was as if all my breath had been suddenly sucked away. I stood and stared.

The valley below us was shaped like a crater, and covered by a huge, frozen lake – a near-perfect circle bordered all the way round by snow-covered mountains. On the far side, a steep snow slope rose to the base of a mountain so much larger than the others that it stuck out like a sore thumb. It towered above them, black and white and bulbous, with a rounded top plunging to sheer sides that looked impossible to climb.

This was it. We'd arrived.

"Kailas," I gasped.

32

It was so strange to finally see it. To be honest, I'd expected something more. The most important mountain in the world, sacred to over a billion people. But Kailas was just a mountain, and not even a very impressive one.

Tenzin obviously didn't feel that way. The moment he saw it he sank to his knees and began to chant. I left him to it; we were well hidden under the canopy of prayer flags, so it was a good spot to plan a route to the mountain's base.

I slid on my smart-goggles and scanned the landscape with the zoom lenses. It was getting darker, the sinking sun glittering the mountain tops with bronze and gold, but there was still enough light to see around the valley. It seemed like the coast was clear – it should have been; no one else knew our destination – but I didn't allow myself to relax. The most dangerous moments usually came when the coast seemed clear.

Tenzin joined me gazing at the Crystal Mountain. I'd never seen such a smile! He was a world-champion grinner, and he shattered his personal best. It was Kailas; just seeing it made him shine.

"Do you know that lake?" I asked.

"Of course. Lake Manasarovar."

"I'm guessing it's sacred?"

"Very sacred."

"Does that mean we can't go near it?"

"No, we must. To bathe in that lake cleanses your sins." Impossibly, his smile spread even wider. "It might be good for you, Manchester United."

I didn't take the bait. There was no way anyone could bathe in that lake; the ice must have been a metre thick. But we could walk across it. The only other way to Kailas was to hike around it – at least a day's effort, but probably longer in such deep snow.

I could hear my mum in my head, insisting we went the long way. That was the safe route, the sensible plan. I just didn't do sensible very well.

I focused my lenses on the lake's far shore, and the steep slope that rose to the base of Kailas. Hills lined it on either side. One of them was dotted with chortens; at least a hundred of them clustered around a small, whitewashed building that looked out over the lake. A trail of smoke rose from the building's chimney.

"What's that place?" I asked.

"Chui Gompa," Tenzin replied. "It is for pilgrims on the way to Kailas. We can stay there for the night."

"It looks like someone's already there."

"No, its fire always burns. Every morning a monk comes to make tea for anyone who arrives."

He seemed certain it was safe, but I wasn't convinced. I switched my goggles to thermal view, and then infrared, but the monastery was too far away to get a reading. It was getting dark, and it would be a perfect rest stop before continuing up the slope to Kailas. But I had a bad feeling about the place, and I'd come to trust those feelings.

I was about to ask more about it, but Tenzin looked back in the direction we had come. His face changed, his smile replaced by a scowl, as he scoured the landscape like a soldier on watch.

"Manchester United..." he breathed. "Do you feel it?"

I stared at him, confused. The only thing I felt was the ache in my legs from the climb. But I'd learned to take Tenzin seriously when he stopped smiling.

"Feel what?" I asked.

"It is back," he hissed. "It is watching us."

I looked in every direction at pristine white slopes. "What, Tenzin? What's watching us?"

"The guardian of the mountain. Why does it follow us, Manchester United? You are not going to climb Kailas." He looked at me, his eyes suddenly full of uncertainty. "Are you?"

230

I swallowed hard, trying not to show anything other than outrage at the question. Part of me still wondered if the guardian spirit was just a spook story to scare me away from the mountain. But another part wasn't so sure.

"We're going to find your chorten," I said. "So we need to cross that lake. It's the quickest way to Kailas."

"To the chorten, you mean?"

I nodded, too eagerly, and tried to change the subject. "Where is it, anyway, this chorten?"

I handed him the goggles, which he ordered to zoom to scan the hill where the monastery sat. All of the chortens looked the same to me, but Tenzin must have spotted the one dedicated to his monastery's founder, because he squealed with delight.

"I see it! Manchester United, I see it!"

He shoved the goggles into my hand and scampered off down the slope. "Let's go!"

I hissed at him to slow down, but seeing the chorten had given him a double dose of energy, and he already had twice as much as me, so he was off like a skidoo. He whooped as he ran, like a child on a school snow day.

The snow deepened from ankle-deep to knee-high as I trudged after him down the hill. I followed in the trench he had carved, but each step was still exhausting.

Suddenly Tenzin stopped. He crouched in the snow and stared across the slope. Something was moving towards us. The grey haze of dusk had settled across the valley, but I could just make out six figures in sheepskins and scarves, struggling around the shore of the lake.

I caught up with Tenzin and dragged him down lower as we watched the group trudge closer. We could hear them now, a rhythmic chanting that echoed up the slope.

"Om mani padme hum. Om mani padme hum..."

"They are pilgrims," Tenzin explained. "On a holy journey to Kailas."

"Are we safe?" I asked.

Tenzin didn't answer, but I wasn't going to trust them just because they seemed to be pilgrims. That would be a perfect disguise for a hunter, after all.

We waited for half an hour, watching the group rest by the frozen lake. They made a yak-dung fire and huddled around it chanting and singing. Nothing about them seemed suspicious; as far as I could tell, they really were pilgrims. The more I thought about it, the more this seemed an excellent opportunity.

"Let's say hello," I suggested.

Tenzin grabbed my arm. "We cannot."

"Why not?"

"They are pilgrims, Manchester United. They have walked many miles to cleanse their sin. We cannot involve them in our activities."

"We're not involving them, we'll just walk with them. It's a good cover."

"Cover?"

"We'll look like part of their group."

"It is a lie. It shrouds them with impurity."

"Come on, Tenzin, it doesn't shroud them with anything. I bet they fancy a bit of company. A break from all that *om-mani-padme-humming*."

I knew Tenzin would protest again, so I didn't give him a chance. I jumped up and set off once more down the hill, waving my arms in signal.

They were cool, too, those pilgrims. At first they were startled to see us, but after a lot of smiling and tashi deleks, they invited us to join them at the fire. Only one of them spoke English, but he spoke it really well.

They were delighted to meet Tenzin – on a pilgrimage, bumping into a monk seemed like the best sort of luck. They showed him diaries they had kept of their trip so far, and he prayed with them. One of the group made yak butter tea, which I managed to drink without pulling a face. If nothing else, it was nice to hold something warm.

Tenzin explained about his mission to rebuild Yerpa Gompa, which delighted them, judging by all the claps and grins. He told them I was joining him, which earned me a round of applause too, and I smiled and again felt bad.

They were headed for Chiu Gompa to rest before beginning a pilgrimage around Mount Kailas. First they wanted to bathe in the lake; apparently this was a vital part of their journey. I had no idea how they'd do it: the entire surface was one thick slab. They tried stamping and hurling rocks, but barely made a dent in the ice. Finally one of them suggested they rub themselves on it, which should have the same sin-cleansing results as bathing. Tenzin tried to drag me along too, but I insisted I was happy by the fire.

I *was* happy by the fire – the vicious cold of the Tibetan night had begun to descend, so there was no way I wanted to lie on ice. But that wasn't why I stayed. One of the other pilgrims had too, unconvinced by the ice-bathing plan.

It was the pilgrim who spoke English.

Here, at last, was my chance.

I shifted closer to him, so my back was turned to Tenzin and the ice-bathers. "Can I ask a favour?" I asked.

He grinned as if being asked favours was his favourite thing. I glanced back to the lake, checking Tenzin was busy. The pilgrims had rolled up their chubas and lay flat on the ice, flapping limbs like they were making snow angels.

"Can you translate something for me," I asked, "and write down what it says?"

I feared for a moment that Tenzin had warned him about the Drak Terma, because the guy's smile faltered as he looked at the goggles I pulled from my pocket. He stared at them, then at me, then took them from my hand. It was a weird reaction, but I didn't think about it much then – although later I wished I had.

He put them on, and I told the lenses to show the last photograph they took. My heart was going triple speed. It wasn't just the anticipation of reading the terma. I was breaking a promise. Tenzin would be devastated if he found out.

"Do you see the writing?" I asked as the pilgrim stared at the photograph on the lenses. "What does it say?"

"These are strange words," he muttered.

"But can you translate them?"

I grabbed one of the diaries the pilgrims had shown us, tore a page from the back, and shoved it with a pencil into the man's hand.

"Can you write it down?" I asked.

He did, a few words that I didn't see as I kept watch on Tenzin, who was trudging back from the lake, looking delighted with his little trip. As he caught my eye, the smile dropped from his face. He walked faster, calling out.

"Manchester United? What are you doing?"

I snatched the paper from the pilgrim just as he finished writing, and stuffed in it my pocket. I needed to distract him, to take his mind off what he'd seen.

"Hey," I said. "I want you to keep those goggles, as a gift."

The pilgrim took them off and stared at me. "What? I cannot!"

"Really, you can."

He insisted he couldn't and I insisted he could, and then he grabbed me in a massive hug, and jumped up and danced around in the snow. By then Tenzin was back and looked more confused than ever.

"What is happening?" he asked.

"A gift," I explained. "They've been kind to us."

Tenzin considered this, his eyebrows so low they seemed to slip into his eyes, and then his face erupted in another epic grin.

"Good, Manchester United! Very good! You see, the lake *has* cleansed you!"

I forced a smile and clutched the paper in my pocket. The pilgrim seemed to have forgotten about it as he showed off his new toy to his friends.

The pilgrims were up for crossing the lake, eager to reach the warmth of Chiu Gompa. They packed up their stuff and we followed them to the shore.

The lake surface felt as solid as concrete. Bubbles squirmed at least half a metre below. It seemed safe, but alarm bells were going off in my head. It would be dark by the time we reached the centre of the lake, a mile from land in every direction. I turned, looking at the pass we'd come from and the other surrounding hills. I wished I'd not given my smart-goggles away; I needed their night vision to watch for hunters. But I could hardly ask for them back; if I did, the pilgrim might mention the Drak Terma, and Tenzin would know I'd lied.

I pulled my chuba tighter as freezing wind swept across the ice. For a while the only sounds were the thunk of our boots on the frozen surface and the creaking of ice underfoot, a creepy and threatening noise, like the groan of a ship's timbers. Ahead, one of the pilgrims began chanting again.

After an hour we reached the centre of the lake. Kailas loomed directly ahead, a vast black tower, like a space rocket about to blast off from the top of the slope. I looked back across the ice. Wind swept powdery snow across the lake surface, but nothing else moved. Even so, something was wrong. I had a sense of it, maybe the same sense that made Tenzin so sure we were being followed by the guardian of the mountain.

"Manchester United," Tenzin called. "What is wrong?"

"I don't know," I replied. "We should walk faster, get off this ice."

Only, we couldn't go any faster. Each step had to be carefully placed to avoid tumbling over. And, anyway, I couldn't explain to the pilgrims why I was so scared; they knew nothing about my real story. Maybe there was a way to get them moving *without* explaining?

I ran three steps and skidded, so I slid several metres over the ice, pushed by the wind at my back. One of the pilgrims grinned and did the same, boot-skating much further than me, and suddenly they were all at it, laughing as they skidded over the lake. Tenzin got involved too. His robes blew against him as he ran and slid, ran and slid.

This was better; we were covering the distance much faster, and it was a good distraction from my fears.

"Clear a path," I yelled. "World record slide coming up."

I skidded over the ice, cheering myself on until I came to a breathless stop. I looked back, delighted by the distance I'd skated from the rest of the group.

"Yes!" I cried. "I'd like to see any of you beat—"

The rest of my words got stuck in my throat as I realized no one was watching me. They were all looking back towards the black hills and the smouldering fire we had left on the shore. At first I didn't understand why.

Then I heard.

It sounded like a swarm of bees. A *huge* swarm of bees.

"No..." I gasped.

For a moment I became part of the lake, frozen solid, as I watched a plume of snow rush up from the pass, swept by something more than the wind. The noise grew louder, and then it appeared, black and terrible against the night.

A drone.

It was far bigger than those that destroyed the monastery. Even from a mile away I could see that it was rigged with weapons and cameras.

All I could do was stare, paralyzed by the realization that we were trapped in the middle of a frozen lake, five hundred metres from the shore. My words, when they finally came, were a whisper from cracked lips.

"Run... Everybody run."

33

Running on ice is easy when you're mucking about, but when you really *need* to run it's different. I slipped, staggered and tumbled back, cracking my head against the rock-hard surface.

Rolling over, I saw Tenzin and the pilgrims charging towards me, snatching terrified glances over their shoulders. The drone swept down the mountainside. Lights flashed on its body, angry red flashes against the slope. The down-draft of its rotors caused rocks to tumble and tiny snow tornadoes to twist up from the ground. I could just see some of the kit rigged to its frame: infrared cameras, heat sensors, robotic grab claws and things that looked worryingly like rocket launchers. They twisted and turned, seeking us out.

I screamed at the pilgrims to run faster, but they were going as fast as they could. They looked confused as much as scared. They could tell that the drone was a threat, but they had no idea why. In that moment, sprawled on the ice, I remembered Tenzin urging me not to join this group. These pilgrims had struggled for weeks to reach Kailas. Now I had dragged them into a nightmare.

I scrambled up and staggered back, yelling for them to hurry.

"Manchester United!" Tenzin screamed. "What now?"

The drone swept from the slope and over the shore of the lake, causing the frozen surface to shudder and sway. One of the machine's gadgets turned, and something fired.

A fizzing blue laser shot into the lake, punching a hole through the thick surface. Chunks of ice flew up, then a geyser of freezing water. The ice rocked up and down, sending us tumbling. The drone was three hundred metres away. The shot had been a warning; there was no escape.

The pilgrims started running again. Desperate to get off the lake, they charged for its closer eastern shore rather than towards Kailas and Chiu Gompa. Tenzin tried to drag me with them, but I resisted. This hunter was after *me* – not them.

"Tenzin!" I shouted above the noise of the drone's rotors, "go with them, get them safe."

"Yes, Manchester United, let's go."

"No. Whoever's controlling that thing is only after me. You go with them, I go that way."

"No, Manchester United. We stay together."

I shook him off and pushed him after the pilgrims. We didn't speak again; we just locked frantic, desperate eyes. He knew I was right: the longer I was with them, the more danger they were in. This hunter didn't seem to want to kill us, but that didn't mean he wouldn't. The reward on my head was dead or alive, after all.

I turned and ran again, heading for Kailas, as wind and snow rushed at my back. I glanced behind me to see the drone coming after me, not the others. Its facial recognition cameras had identified me, and its laser blaster had me in its sights. Lights flashed more brightly around the machine, as if the drone was excited to close in on its prey.

Another crackling blue blast, a hundred metres away. An explosion of ice and water caused the lake to jolt, flipping me over. It was a second warning shot, and I doubted I'd get many more. I scrambled up and kept running, praying I could make it to the shore.

I heard the angry buzz of the rotors, felt the rush of air against my back. The shadow of the machine swallowed me, and then came another laser blast.

More ice shattered. The lake surface seesawed, catapulting me into the air. Freezing water rained down as I crashed back onto the ice. I didn't have time to get up before the drone fired again, this time ten metres ahead of me. I was flung up again, landed again. Freezing water soaked my chuba, and the raft of ice I was on began to sink. I wiped wet hair from my eyes and stared across the shattered lake. Thick chunks of ice rose up and sank under, and water flooded the slabs that stayed afloat.

Amid the chaos I spotted Tenzin and the pilgrims scrambling to safety at the lake's shore. They had survived; that was something.

The drone circled and fired again, destroying another area of unbroken ice.

My soaked chuba felt as heavy as a bearskin. My body began to shake from the cold. The water was well below freezing; if I fell in I'd die of hypothermia in seconds.

I rose to my knees, staring at the moonlit edge of the lake fifty metres away. Some of the ice ahead was unbroken, but there was no way the hunter would let me reach the shore. Even if I could, what then? The monastery on the hill was close, but the drone would blow it to bits if I hid inside.

Just get there, and then worry about that.

I breathed in deeply, held the breath, and released it slowly, letting my eyes scour the lake's fractured surface. There was always a way out if I could clear my mind of fear. The lake was shattered into icebergs, which I could use as stepping stones to reach the shore. But I had to go now, before the hunter blew them into ice cubes.

I ran and jumped, springing from one slab to

another. The drone fired ahead of me, so I changed my direction and sprang to my side. The blast caused the slab to swing up, but I used the momentum to jump to another, and then another. I kept running, leaping over channels of water between broken ice. My eyes shot and darted, seeking the best path to the shore.

Another blast – metres away – caused a slab to flip up and fire me straight into the air. I belly-flopped down onto ice, but my legs slipped into freezing water. The shock caused my muscles to spasm, so both legs became useless. It was all I could do to cling onto the swaying iceberg.

"Get up, Jake! Get up!"

I thought the voice was in my head, but it called louder.

"Move, Jake! Now!"

I saw Tenzin screaming from the shore. It struck me that it was the first time he'd used my real name.

I rose on weak, shaking legs, struggling to keep my balance on the rocking ice slab. I heard Tenzin cry out again. I heard the buzz of drone rotors. I heard my teeth chattering and the splash and shatter of breaking ice.

I jumped again and again. A laser shot hit another ice slab, which flipped up and launched me into the air once more, flailing my arms. I landed on something soft and sank down, certain I'd hit the water.

But I hadn't. It was snow.

I'd made it to the shore!

The realization gave me fresh energy, and I dragged myself to my feet. I screamed at the drone above me, swearing and threatening, and then kicked away snow and waded up the hill towards the fire-light of Chui Gompa. The snow was windblown and powdery, softer than on the other side of the lake, but there was no way I could outrun this drone.

Now something else fired from the drone – something dark and spidery that hit the snow a few metres to my side. A net!

It had fired from a mini-cannon, loaded with more nets to catch me. Only the drone was moving slower, shaking. A few of its lights had gone out as its motor struggled in the high-altitude air.

Another net fired. I dived into the snow, sank under it and thrust myself forward so I burst up ahead of the net – then did it again as the drone fired another. It felt as if the snow was against me too, trying to pull me down. It would have been easy to let it, but I refused to give up. If I was going to die, I wanted to die somewhere warm.

Through snow-blurred vision I saw the drone shaking harder as it chased me up the hill. A blast of wind slapped it sideways, causing its net cannon to detach and drop to the snow. Now the hunter had to use his laser blaster.

I grabbed the cannon, a titanium tube the length of a baseball bat, and used it as a walking stick to help me through the snow. My vision was so blurred, and my mind so scrambled with fear, that I didn't know I'd reached the monastery until I walked right into its stone wall. I cried out in delight, and staggered along the wall to a wooden door. But the latch was frozen solid. Screaming, I rammed it with the end of the net cannon, shattering the ice so the door swung open.

Inside were Kyle and Veronika Flutes.

For a second we all stared. The hunters, both wrapped in blankets and sitting beside a stove, froze mid-sip of their tea. Veronika's unpatched eye twitched.

I grabbed the door and slammed it shut. Panic hit me like an avalanche. I remember swearing, and almost throwing up with fear. My heart was going too fast and my head was starting to spin, but instinct made me move. I dived to one side just as a bolt of blue fire burst through the door, shattering wood. Kyle Flutes had got his stun gun out.

I dropped the net cannon and staggered back along the side of the monastery. I stumbled around the corner, but all I had left for cover was a few metres of wall. Over frantic, gasping breaths I heard the drone buzzing closer. It could see me with its thermal camera. It was waiting around that corner. But if I stayed where I was, Kyle and Veronika would be on me in moments.

I had to try my luck with the drone. Even at full strength I stood no chance against the hunters, and

I was definitely not at full strength. The drone still sounded like it was struggling with the altitude; the splutter of its motor was now even louder than the whir of its rotors. I had to make a run for it, but where to? I doubted I'd make it five steps before the drone shot me in the back. But that still sounded better than being caught by Kyle and Veronika. I could hear them coming, boots crunching snow, stalking closer...

The buzz of the drone grew even louder. Red lights flashed against snow, just around the corner. Was I really about to charge into its firing line?

My legs were icicles, frozen with fear.

Go, Jake! Run!

I was just about to when I heard something else.

A grunt and a thump.

A stun gun blast fired, a wild, stray shot into the sky. Veronika screamed. *Nothing* frightened Veronika Flutes. And then I heard something more terrifying than hunters or a drone – a roar that tore through the night, shuddering the chamber walls and causing icicles to fall from the roof.

At first I didn't move. I *couldn't* move. The shock of that sound, the fear of its source, had frozen me to the spot. Finally, I edged back to the corner, boots sliding over snow. Very slowly, I peeked around the side of the monastery. What I saw turned my insides into a block of ice.

Kyle and Veronika lay unconscious on the ground. Pieces of Kyle's stun gun lay scattered about the snow, around footprints that were far bigger than any I had ever seen...

My stomach somersaulted and my mouth was parched with fear. What had just happened?

Behind me the drone flew closer. Jumping over Kyle and Veronika, I staggered back into the monastery. The room looked like those at Tenzin's old home, with silk banners on the walls and pillows on the floor for praying. It had the same hatch in the roof, and the same slide ladder to reach it. A pot of yak butter tea simmered over the stove. I rushed to it and pressed myself against the cauldron, groaning with pleasure as warmth soaked into my legs.

Outside, the drone fired another shot, close enough to the chamber to act as a warning: come out or die. The cauldron shook and hot tea sloshed down my chest. The liquid scalded me, but the burn helped focus my mind. For a few seconds I stood still in the middle of the chamber, feeling my breath rise and fall. I closed my eyes. The storm in my head began to calm. My eyes opened, and I knew what to do.

I darted to the door and grabbed the net cannon. Then I scrambled back to the stove, grabbed two sacks from beside the fire – one with yak butter and the other full of yak dung – and shoved handfuls of one into the other. Swinging the net cannon, I managed to unhook the ladder from the ceiling. I clambered up, carrying the dung-butter mix and the cannon.

I curled my back into the roof hatch and barged

it open, letting in a rush of snow and freezing wind. The drone spotted me the moment I appeared on the monastery roof, its searchlight swivelling and glaring. The machine swooped closer and lower, coming straight at me.

Trying not to panic, I scooped a handful of the dung-butter mix and stuffed it down the barrel of the net cannon. It was a simple weapon – a tube and a trigger – so all I had to do was point and shoot, but the recoil sent me staggering back to the edge of the roof. I looked up and saw my shot miss the drone.

The machine rushed closer.

I stuffed another wad of dung-butter into the cannon, fired again – and missed again. I cursed and loaded another scoop. My hands were trembling so hard I could barely hold the weapon. I glanced up and saw the drone shooting straight for me.

Come on, Jake, get this right!

I breathed in, held my breath and fired.

The dung-butter mix splatted across the drone's camera. The machine fired a laser blast, but without its camera the shot missed me by metres. I staggered to the side of the roof as the drone fired again, and missed again. The hunter couldn't see me, but a bit of yak dung wasn't going to stop this thing. I had to make this count. I braced myself to time this right...

Snow swirled up from the roof. The machine rushed low over the monastery, red lights flashing and robotic grab claws snapping. Its laser cannon turned and fired, but it was just a hopeful shot that missed me at the side of the roof. I waited ... and then ran and leaped onto the drone.

Then things got *really* crazy.

I landed on top of it and clung onto whatever I could. One of the rotors sliced my arm, snapped and pinged off into the sky. The others kept spinning as the drone carried me up and away from the monastery. Still wrapped around it, I yanked at mechanical parts, tearing wires, pulling off another rotor. But the thing kept flying, taking me up higher. I was thirty feet above the slope when the drone finally started to splutter. One of its rotors was still spinning, but its motor was struggling. Lights plinked out.

Then we started to drop.

I slipped off the machine and fell. I pinned my arms to my sides, locked my legs together and prayed the snow was soft and thick enough to catch me. I hit it feet first and sank. Panic kicked in before I'd stopped sinking. I scrabbled around, trying to climb back up, but the snow closed in, trapping me. I screamed, fighting to escape, but I only sank deeper into the snow. I sucked a last breath as the snow covered my face, blocking my nose and mouth, suffocating me.

There was nothing I could do. There was no plan to get out of this. I tried to scream now, but my mouth filled with snow.

This was it. This was where I died.

The cold numbed me, so it didn't hurt. Mainly, I was embarrassed. This was my fault. I was so close to Kailas, right at its base. So close to the answers, the secrets we'd gone through so much to uncover...

The snow pressed harder against my face, and I closed my eyes. I swear that I saw her face: her pale, sunken cheeks and ruby-red lips, curled into a smirk. Marjorie. The Snake Lady.

Had she won?

34

A chink of light.

Something bright, something other than the darkness of the deep snow. My frozen eyelids cracked open, blurrily aware of a yellow light in my face, filtering through the snow.

I couldn't breathe.

The light grew even brighter. My heart surged with hope, but surely whoever was coming was too late.

Please... Please...

I heard voices calling out, urgent.

A hand scraped snow from my face, forced my mouth open, and dug more from inside. I gasped a desperate breath. The torchlight was in my eyes, dazzling me. Had I been saved or caught?

More hands appeared, dragging me from my snow tomb. It could have been hunters, or the Snake Lady's goons, but I let them take me. There was nothing I could do. The cold had sucked the energy from every part of my body.

The hands laid me on a blanket. Blurry shapes crowded round. Someone slapped me around the face. A second slap struck sense back into me. I reached out a shaky hand and wiped the snow from my eyes, trying to focus on the looming figures. The torchlight cut out and I realized what it had been – not just a torch: *smart-goggles*.

My eyes focused on a face – it was the pilgrim I'd given the goggles to. All of his group were here; they had saved me! One of them slapped me again.

I rose a little, shivering and mumbling thank yous.

"Shall I hit you again?" the pilgrim asked.

"No... I... How did you find me?"

The pilgrim's grin spread wider and he tapped the smart-goggles. "Thermal camera," he said. "You do not want these back, do you?"

I shook my head. The goggles were the least I owed him. I sat up further and gazed around the hill as my eyes adjusted to the night. A grey trail of smoke rose a short distance down the slope where the drone had crashed into one of the chortens. There was a figure there, silhouetted against snow and smoke.

"Tenzin?" I rasped.

The pilgrim pointed to the boy monk. "Tenzin sad," he said.

I rubbed my legs, bringing enough life back into them to stand, although I still felt like I might collapse at any moment. I staggered through the snow to where Tenzin sat among a pile of rocks.

"Hey," I called. "You OK?"

He didn't seem to hear.

"Tenzin?"

Still no reply, but he didn't seem to be praying. I waded closer. "Tenzin?"

"Go away, Jake."

His voice was soft, a whisper. Was he angry at me for involving the pilgrims in this? "Hey, I'm sorry, I shouldn't have—"

"I said go away!"

Whoa. I hadn't known Tenzin long, but I'd never heard him talk with so much rage. Did he know that I had asked the pilgrim to translate the Drak Terma? If so, then he must have guessed I still planned to find the Hall of Records.

I shuffled closer, and was about to speak again when I realized what he was sitting on – not rocks, but rubble. It was the stone base of a chorten, all that was left of one that the drone had destroyed as it fell.

And then I understood.

Not *a* chorten. *His* chorten.

It was the memorial Tenzin had come to pray at for permission to rebuild his monastery. But now it was ruined too.

"Tenzin, I'm sorry. That was bad luck. I didn't know that would happen."

"No," he replied, without turning. "But it did. It happened because of you, Jake."

Jake. I wanted him to smile, to call me Manchester United. But I knew what he meant. Not just the chorten, but his monastery and the pilgrims' journey to Kailas. I had wreaked havoc right here at the holiest place in his world.

I gazed up to the sheer face of Kailas. The wind was rising, whipping flurries of snow across the slope that rose to the mountain's base.

"Tenzin, we can still do something good. The Drak Terma, it's—"

I didn't know what I was going to say, but I didn't get a chance. Tenzin whirled around, his eyes wild with an anger I doubted he'd known before. He marched up to me and yelled so close that specks of spit hit my cheeks.

"No! You are *not* sorry," he seethed. "You are not sorry about anything. You do not care about me or my monastery, or anything but your mission. You just pretend, to get what you want."

"That's not true..."

"It is! You have been shown nothing but kindness. By all of those people you planned to betray."

His eyes watered as he struggled to fight tears. He was a monk, dedicated to peace. This anger confused him as much as it surprised me.

"You are no different to other treasure hunters," he spat.

"That's not true. They're the bad guys, Tenzin."

"*You* are the bad guy, Jake! All the things you destroyed. All the promises you have broken. For what? To find treasure, to beat others."

"No, I told you I came here to help you..."

He lashed out again, shoving me so I tumbled back to the snow.

"Another lie!" he shouted. "You think I do not know? You already have the Drak Terma. Were you even going to help me rebuild my home at all?"

I couldn't answer – I didn't *know* the answer. I stared up at Tenzin, his slight, shaking frame dwarfed by the black bulk of the mountain. Tears slid down his cheeks and dripped to the snow. His fists unclenched and his shoulders slumped, rage replaced by defeat. He sank to his knees beside me in the snow.

"What is the point of finding treasure," he gasped, "when you have lost your soul?"

At that moment a searchlight caught us both in a wide glare. Now another, and another – three fierce spotlights targeting us from helicopters that seemed to appear from nowhere. We'd been so lost in our fight that neither of us had noticed their approach. Voices boomed from speakers, commands I neither heard nor cared about. We weren't going to run. For Tenzin, there was no point – his chorten was destroyed, his journey was over. I could have tried to carry on; I had the information I needed in my pocket, after all. But I was drained. I had nothing left.

Engines revved, and I was vaguely aware of snow-mobiles speeding closer. I had no idea who had caught us, just that we *were* caught. There was no escape, not now.

As the lights rushed closer, I stared up at the Crystal Mountain, this vast lump of rock and ice that meant so much to so many people. With my last scraps of energy, I reached into my pocket, dug out the paper with the translation of the Drak Terma, and read what it said in the searchlight glare. Then I tore it up and tossed the pieces into the wind.

I whispered two words. I'm not sure who they were for: my family, Tenzin, or maybe just for the mountain.

"I'm sorry."

35

Marjorie had to be careful.

Her guide – the smiling but silent Tibetan she had hired to take her to Mount Kailas – had driven as far as he said was possible. She knew how sacred this mountain was to the people of this land; the guide had told her at least a dozen times on the journey from Lhasa. He had been particularly pleased when she claimed she was a pilgrim making a holy journey to Kailas. Each time they passed prayer wheels by the roadside he'd suggested they stopped to pray, but she'd always refused and eventually the man had grown suspicious. Why would a pilgrim *not* pray? She had tried to placate him with false sentiments – "my heart only lies at Kailas," or "only at the Crystal Mountain may I seek forgiveness for my sins" – and they had worked for a while. But after three days, the guide had decided that she was up to something, that it had nothing to do with religion, and that he wanted no part of it.

He would leave her at the next village, twenty kilometres from Kailas. She had hoped to convince him to take her further – she really did not want to walk twenty kilometres in this snow – but when they arrived they discovered they could not *go* any further.

Something was happening at Kailas, the villagers said.

Something strange, they said.

They had seen helicopters – huge, black beasts – and jeeps, and men that looked like the army but they did not think *were* the army.

Marjorie knew then that the Atlas family had been caught. She had no idea how, or by whom. Perhaps a hunter had bagged the reward, or maybe Lord Osthwait had succeeded where she had failed. It didn't really matter. Jake was there, at the mountain. So that's where she was going too.

She paid a villager for an extra shawl so that she was eight layers deep against the freeze. Then she set off on the hike, her hands shoved in her pockets as much for warmth as to grip the phurba knife with which she would kill the boy. Reaching him wouldn't be easy, but if Lord Osthwait had been too busy to cancel her credit cards, perhaps he had also failed to inform the mercenaries that she had been removed from the operation. They might not know. She might have a chance.

But, still, she had to be careful.

36

"Jake Montgomery Atlas."

That was a low blow, using my middle name, but I didn't react. I sat staring up at the cone-shaped mountain as moonlight gleamed off its plunging glaciers, frozen waterfalls and wind-polished rock. It was beautiful, mesmerizing, as if Kailas's vast western face was studded with crystals.

But despite how far I had come to reach this place, I wished I were anywhere else. To make it worse, I had to listen to this idiot.

Tall, posh and English, he spoke like one of the Royal Family. He'd arrived in a military helicopter, along with forty mercenary goons dressed in black snowsuits, parkas and winter boots.

The guy wore a stupid hat with spaniel earflaps, and the biggest fur coat I'd ever seen. It looked like he'd skinned a bear. The weight of the thing troubled him, and he leaned on a trekking pole to stop himself from toppling forward. He'd managed to find a spot on the coat to pin a brooch. It was the same ornament the Snake Lady wore: the emerald snake eating its own tail. He was one of the People of the Snake – not a goon; someone senior.

He cleared his throat and wiped a drip of snot from his nose with a mitten. "Do you know who I am?" he asked.

I shook my head vaguely.

"Do you know *why* you do not know who I am?" he asked.

I shrugged even more vaguely.

"Because we are a secret organization," he continued. "*Top* secret. Now, do you know how I know who *you* are?"

I sighed. "I really don't care."

I think he had a speech planned, to make sure I knew I was caught. It wasn't necessary. I knew. I was broken, bleeding and exhausted. The mercenaries had handcuffed me to a rail on one of their helicopters at the base of the slope to Kailas. It must have been past midnight, and I'd not rested properly in days, but I couldn't sleep. For at least an hour I'd sat staring out of the helicopter's open side, up the steep slope to the mountain. Now this guy was in the way.

"I am going to ask you two questions," he said. "How you are treated from this point will depend on your answers."

"Don't bother," I muttered. "I'm not going to tell you what the Drak Terma said. Where's Marjorie, anyway? She was way better at this stuff than you. She was properly scary. You look like an awkward teddy bear."

"Number nine has been removed from this operation."

"Number nine?"

"Marjorie."

That was weird to hear. I hated that woman, but what my sister claimed was true; I had become obsessed with her, or with beating her to the end of this hunt. She was the face of our enemy, but now she wasn't even here.

"What's your second question?" I asked.

"Where are your family?"

Whoa. Now he had my attention. This whole time I had thought they had been caught, but that obviously wasn't the case...

"Where are they?" he demanded. "Tell me."

I got the feeling he was used to people answering when he barked at them. I leaned closer, as far as I could with the handcuffs.

"Disneyland," I replied.

"I... What?"

"I wanted to come here, but I was outvoted, so they went to Disneyland."

"I don't believe you."

"Disney World? Which one is in Florida?"

"You're not as clever as you think you are."

"I don't think I'm clever at all. You wouldn't either if you lived with my parents and sister."

I shifted, gazing past him to the operation centre that his mercenaries had set up across the slope, a hundred metres from the base of the mountain. Those goons may have been slow at catching their enemies, but they could set up a high-tech military-style field headquarters in no time. They'd pitched tents, rigged lights and generators, and positioned satellite dishes. Holospheres projected 3D images of Mount Kailas, which seemed unnecessary with the real thing right above them.

None of it mattered; without the Drak Terma they had no idea where to look for the Hall of Records.

I shifted to see in the other direction, hoping I might see Tenzin on the hill to Chiu Gompa. Had he left, or was he still there, by the ruins of his chorten? I remembered his excitement when we left his village, how proud he'd been to be on a mission to rebuild his monastery, and how happy that I was joining him. Now he knew that had been a lie. I wanted to talk to him, but I couldn't let this old guy know I knew him; he might use that against me. And, anyway, what would I say? I had a new mission, and once again it didn't involve helping Tenzin.

From the moment I heard my family were free, I had to escape. If they were still being hunted, I had to help them. If I could beat the People of the Snake to the end of this quest, I could use whatever I found to make this guy call off the hunt. First I needed a few minutes to think.

I'd read the Drak Terma before I was caught. The pilgrim who translated it had scribbled just two words: *ENTER TEETH*.

It was strange, but made a sort of sense. I remembered Pan's lesson about sacred Buddhist symbols that represented parts of the body. There had been a symbol for teeth – a conch shell. So the Drak Terma was guiding me to a conch shell in the mountain, or something that *looked* like a conch shell...

I'd spotted it already. Beyond the mercenaries' camp, at the top of the slope, there was a cave opening into the base of Mount Kailas. The cave mouth was shaped like a conch shell – or maybe an upside down teardrop – with a sliver at ground level, just a crack in the rock, rising to a larger opening above.

Maybe I'd read the clue wrong, but my family had solved a few secret codes recently, and I was beginning to get an instinct for them. Somehow I just knew; that cave was my destination. Inside it I would find a way into the mountain, to the Hall of Records.

"So what now?" I asked him.

He snorted in a I-think-that-should-be-perfectly-obvious sort of way, but then looked confused, as if on second thoughts he wasn't sure either. He'd been desperate to catch me, but didn't have a clue what happened next.

He dug his trekking pole harder into the snow. "We have ways to make you talk," he said. "You have no idea of the resources we have to—"

"I do!" I cried. "I do have an idea! I know all about your resources. I just *don't care*. You've caught me, see, handcuffs! It's embarrassing to stand around gloating. I'm not going to give you the Drak Terma and I'm not going to give up my family. So just carry on with whatever it is you're doing. I'll sit here and look at the mountain."

He sneered at me a few times and huffed a little, but then pulled his coat tighter and trudged off to one of his operation tents. I waited until I was sure he wasn't looking and then got busy trying to escape.

37

This had been easier than she expected. Not the journey, which had been difficult enough, but getting in among the organization's operation. It had been a doddle.

It felt strange, though. She had approached with confidence, so any mercenary who knew she had been ousted from the council might be disarmed simply by her presence. Fooling these thugs didn't take much effort. Rather, it felt strange because this was no longer *hers*. As she approached the first operation tent, Marjorie wasn't scared. Rather, she was overcome with loss and anger. She was a mother watching someone else raise her children.

It was the anger that burned the brightest. This moment, this culmination of everything she had worked for – everything she had sacrificed – should be hers. She reached into her coat pocket and gripped the phurba, letting its blade sting her skin. But one pain did not soothe the other. This should be hers and it wasn't, and that was all the fault of—

She stopped beyond the tent. A few mercenaries spotted her and began to work harder, flicking through files on a holosphere. They were attempting to impress her whilst at the same time failing spectacularly at their job. She barely noticed them. Her gaze was fixed on something else, something beyond the tent, fifty metres away by the frozen lake.

A helicopter.

Sitting in it, caught and cuffed, was Jake Atlas.

And the rage roared louder.

She kept moving, her hand so tight against the blade that it sliced her palm and drew its first blood.

38

I tugged at the cuffs until skin tore on my wrist and blood slid from beneath the steel shackles. I'd hoped they had been built for adults, and a skinny-wristed kid like me would be able to wriggle free. But it was as if they had been made especially for me.

If I couldn't get out of these cuffs myself, maybe someone else would do it for me. The People of the Snake needed me alive for the information I had on the Drak Terma. If I could cause a fire or an explosion, they'd be forced to release me. I had no idea how I'd reach the cave – I'd have to get right through their camp – but I could worry about that once I was free.

I shifted as far around as the cuffs would let me, scanning for anything in the helicopter that might cause a fire. There was a control panel in the wall, knobs and dials that meant nothing to me other than that they might explode. I yanked again at the cuffs, gritting my teeth as their metal edge dug into my skin. My boot heel was inches from the panel; surely a few hard kicks would do the job...

"I would not do that if I were you," a voice said.

I froze, my heel hovering an inch from the panel. It was as if I'd been shot by one of the mercenaries' stun guns, causing every muscle in my body to tense and stop working – paralyzing me.

"Hello, Jake," the voice added.

My mind drained of every useful thought, every clever plan. Right then, all I knew was a name.

Slowly, I turned my head.

"Hello, Marjorie," I croaked.

39

He looked remarkably healthy, considering the journey he must have had. A few bruises, many scratches and a cut on his arm that needed stitches. That wasn't a bad return against an open hunt across one of the wildest landscapes in the world. She had always admired that about the boy – he was a survivor.

But, oh, his face when he saw her! It was like he had been hit by a snowball in the middle of the summer: shock and confusion. Marjorie clenched her jaw to stop herself from grinning.

Wait until he sees the knife.

Her hand remained tight around the weapon hidden in her coat pocket. Still, she was a little disappointed. Jake's plan to escape seemed to involve vandalizing the helicopter and little else. She had come to expect more from the boy.

"That panel is the automatic door seal," she explained. "If it fails, the helicopter door will close, trapping you inside. I'm not sure that would aid your escape."

He swore at her, which was unnecessary, and then spat at her, which was just crude. Was this really the same boy she had once hoped to recruit into the organization?

"What do you want?" he snapped. "That old guy said you were gone."

She gripped the knife handle even tighter. This was a tricky situation. Jake had shifted back, so she would have to climb into the helicopter to use the knife. He was well positioned to stop her with his feet, which he seemed eager to use. But if she could get him away from this place, she could take her time.

40

Come on... Come closer, you witch.

My legs were tensed, ready to strike. Just one hard kick to her nose. It wouldn't help me escape, but it would be a tiny bit of revenge for everything this woman had done to my family. I could tell she was fighting a smirk, and I wanted to boot it off her face. But she stepped back, shoved her hand into her parka and pulled the coat tighter against the cold. Frost glistened in her snow-coloured hair. It surprised me to see her shiver – this seemed the perfect place for an ice queen.

She sighed, a cloud that shimmered in the moonlight. "You are right," she said. "I have been removed from this operation."

"Good riddance," I grunted. "Who's that posh guy that spoke to me?"

"Lord Osthwait? He is here?"

"Yeah. He actually caught me, which you never could."

"Because I didn't want to."

I lowered my legs, aware they looked silly hovering in the air.

"Darling Jake..."

"Oh, stop it," I groaned. "Stop it with your 'darlings' and sugary talk. You're a cold-hearted cow, Marjorie. You've tried to kill my family a dozen times."

"Yes. Each of those was, I believed, heartbreakingly necessary. An end that justified its terrible means. Your actions put the organization's entire plan at risk. There was no other way of stopping you."

I sat up, yanking against my cuffs so that I faced her. She had probably been sent to talk me into revealing the Drak Terma, so I needed to watch my words. She was far smarter than me. I had to keep insulting her until she gave up and went away, so I could concentrate on getting to that cave.

"Your 'plan' involved killing millions, Marjorie."

Her eyes seemed to turn black, like a snowman's, as if she'd been injected with rage. She blinked, and breathed another frost cloud.

"Controlled depopulation," she admitted. "It is controversial, yes."

"Controversial? That's like Hitler saying the First World War was a 'bit dodgy.' You're crazy and we're going to stop you."

"*Second* World War."

273

"What?"

"Hitler. The *Second* World War."

"Oh, shut your face and get lost. Go tell Lord Snooty that he's not getting the Drak Terma no matter who he sends over."

"Jake, listen to me."

"No."

"I want to help you."

"Then go jump in a crevasse."

"I want to help you escape."

41

That got him. He had been doing so well. She had felt proud of him. His attitude was vulgar, but his defiance was admirable. Of course he was scared – that was clear from his eyes and the tremble in his voice – but he'd tried to hide it.

His family were obviously his chief concern. Marjorie guessed that he still hoped to save them, probably by finding the Hall of Records in this mountain. But he couldn't escape alone. He could spit and swear all he liked, but he needed her help.

"I want to help you, Jake," she repeated.

He swore again, but his eyes flicked past her to the operation tents as if checking if the mercenaries had heard. He was confused. She needed to press her advantage.

"Jake, listen to me."

"No, you shut your—"

"Just listen to me for once. Everything you said is true. Controlled depopulation is wrong. I was part of a council, the leaders of the organization, but I turned against them. I came to realize that the end didn't justify the means. They couldn't pick and choose who lived and died."

His own words spat back out at him, and his eyes changed. Just a flicker of uncertainty, the trickle that freezes and cracks the stone. Again she fought a smile.

"Please, Jake, just listen. I'm not asking you to forgive me. I'm simply offering help. The cataclysm that wiped out the lost civilization *will* come again. The Hall of Records may tell us how and when. People deserve to know. You and your family are the only hope for that. This moment decides which way it goes."

"Why should I believe you? First Lord What's-his-face tries to get the Drak Terma, then he sends you to try. I'm not falling for it."

"I'm not asking you to. I'm just going to give you a key."

"What key?"

"The key to those cuffs."

42

Oh, man, this was tricky.

There was no way I believed her, but I wasn't sure it was *all* lies. The way she kept glancing at the mercenaries... She looked genuinely scared of being caught. And in general she seemed different. Less cocky and smug, her hands constantly shoved in her pockets instead of sweeping the air with their usual theatrical flourishes. She looked weaker too, a little broken. I'd never seen that in her; usually she bossed those mercenaries around like they were school children, barking orders between smug, self-satisfied grins.

And I needed that key. She had placed it in front of me on the floor of the helicopter, a skeleton key like those I'd used on other missions – a pen-sized tube with picks and a laser scanner that "decoded" any lock.

I knew this was a trap. They planned to follow me to wherever the Drak Terma led, but that was fine if they were just *following*. I would still get there first. I could threaten to destroy whatever I found unless they called off the hunt on my family. It wasn't a great plan, but I'd be better off than stuck here cuffed to a helicopter.

She was studying me with those marble eyes. She thought she was in charge. OK, if it got me out of these cuffs I'd go along with her for now. And then I'd change the rules.

Actually, things had just got a little easier. I still had to get to the cave, only now I knew they would *let me* get there. Two of the mercenaries' snowmobiles had been left suspiciously close to the helicopter. Their headlights were beaming. Was that for my benefit, signalling my escape route?

"Do you know how to ride one of those?" I asked.

Marjorie followed my gaze and her face grew even paler. "Don't be ridiculous," she replied. "We can't use those."

"They're our only escape," I insisted. "As soon as I'm out of these cuffs, we need to run. If we get lucky we'll make it to those snowmobiles."

Her lips screwed up tight as she stared at the machines. She was acting, and she was good at it. She looked horrified, and she hadn't heard the *really* mad bit yet...

"Once we get them started," I explained, "we have to drive straight at those mercenaries."

"*What?*"

"That's the way we have to go: right through their camp."

"That's the way the Drak Terma directed you? But to where?"

I glanced at her, knowing she was fishing for information. "You'll find out if you're coming."

"But... We'll never make it."

She sounded properly scared. There were forty mercenaries in that camp, all armed with stun guns. They'd brought other weapons too, although I had no idea *what* weapons. The last I'd seen of Lord Osthwait, he'd been yelling at some goons carrying a wooden crate, warning them of the danger of its contents. There were two of those crates – some sort of cannons, I guessed, to blast a path into the mountain. But I didn't think they were about to use *those* against us.

Marjorie kept muttering about the plan, but I didn't listen as I breathed in deeply, held the breath and let it go. My mind became as clear as the high altitude air, my thoughts sharp and focused.

"Let's go," I said.

The cuffs opened easily with the skeleton key, leaving blood bracelets on my wrists. My hands had turned blue and were almost numb from the pain of the shackles, but there was no time to worry about that.

I jumped out of the helicopter, shoulder-barged Marjorie to the snow and ran. I knew the mercenaries would let me reach the snowmobiles, but I didn't want to let on that I'd sussed their plan. I acted like I was in a panic, charging along one of the trenches they'd carved in the snow. I was halfway there when I heard the first shout.

"Hey! He's free!"

The goon sounded genuinely surprised. I made it to the snowmobile, jumped on and fumbled with the controls, trying to suss out how to get the thing started. I'd driven quad bikes before and this seemed similar, only with two skis at the front for steering and a crawler track at the back.

I grabbed the handlebars and was about to turn the throttle when a stun blast fired from the camp, missing me by inches. I tumbled off the snowmobile.

"Hey!" I screamed. "That almost hit me!"

"Jake! Get down!"

I wiped the snow from my eyes and saw Marjorie stagger closer. She looked terrified, so pale I could see the veins in her face.

"Take cover!" she wailed.

"Why?" I called. "No one's going to shoot—"

Another stun blast fizzed past my face, so close that hairs crackled on my head. What were these guys doing? Lord Osthwait stumbled from one of the tents, roaring orders at the goons. In seconds all the mercenaries were in action mode, grabbing weapons and charging at us.

Something worrying occurred to me...

"Jake!" Marjorie screamed. "Get that machine working!"

She dived to the snow as one of the goons fired again – a shot that hit the ground, spraying up snow. Another struck the snowmobile that I was sheltering behind. Sparks scattered, and smoke billowed from the engine as the machine caught fire. I scrambled away from it and hurled myself behind the second snowmobile.

Marjorie crawled up beside me, coughing from the smoke. Stun blasts streaked past us as the mercenaries charged closer.

"Why aren't they letting me escape?" I demanded.

"Why would they let you escape?" she spluttered. "Wait, do you think this is a set-up?"

"Of course it's a set-up! You're letting me escape to follow me, aren't you? Please say yes!"

She didn't need to tell me I was wrong – the mercenaries had confirmed it with their attack. This *wasn't* a set-up. Did that mean Marjorie was telling the truth, that she really *was* on my side? It didn't matter; either way I had to reach the cave beyond the camp. The stun blasts hadn't taken out the second snowmobile, so I still had a chance. A very *slim* chance, but that would do for now.

Mercenaries stalked closer, screaming at us to surrender. They must have thought we were armed or they'd have grabbed us by now.

"Does this snowmobile have any weapons?" I asked.

"What?" Marjorie gasped.

"Does it have any weapons?"

"What?"

"Stop staying what! A stun gun, something like that?"

"Yes, on the front. A high-intensity plasma focused—"

"Great," I interrupted. "Are you ready?"

"What?"

"Seriously, stop saying that! Come on!"

I leaped onto the snowmobile and grabbed the handlebars. One hard twist got the engine going, and another thrust the machine forward as Marjorie scrambled onto the back. The steering was more sensitive than I'd expected, and at first we drove in a hectic zigzag, skidding and spraying up snow. The mercenaries had no idea where to aim, so they started scatter-shooting across the slope, hoping to get lucky. Plasma blasts fired all around us, as if we were trapped in the middle of a fireworks display. One of the shots struck the back of the snowmobile in an explosion of sparks.

"My coat's on fire!" Marjorie shrieked.

"What do you expect me to do about that?" I yelled.

"Put it out!"

"I'm driving!"

"Let me off; I've changed my mind!"

I would gladly have let her off, but there was no time to stop. I kept yanking the handlebars, forcing sharp turns to disrupt the mercenaries' aim. At the same time I bashed the dashboard controls. There were only a few buttons and dials, so eventually I hit the right one and a shot fired from the front of the snowmobile. The blast was so powerful it caused the whole machine to jolt.

Marjorie clung on even tighter, wrapping me in a bear hug that made it tricky to steer. I tried to shove her off, but she refused to let go. My shot had fired across the slope, missing the mercenaries, but causing panic.

I turned the snowmobile and fired again. The second shot slammed into the side of one of the tents. Now the canvas caught fire and Lord Osthwait freaked out, screaming at the goons to put out the flames. That surprised me; surely he wanted them to catch me rather than save an old tent? Then I remembered the crates he'd been so scared of his goons dropping...

"Marjorie!" I screamed.

"Let me off!"

"Shut up and listen! What's in those two crates?"

"I don't know!"

"So look!"

"They're electrothermal plasma cannons."

"Will they blow up?"

"Wait, why? Jake, please say you're not going to do what I think you are?"

"You sound like my mum, Marjorie."

I turned and drove straight for the burning tent.

Mercenaries opened fire but I ducked low and the shots flew past. I fired again, and then again and again – each shot aimed at the burning tent. I sent five plasma blasts into the flames, before I turned sharply and accelerated away across the slope.

I heard Lord Osthwait scream. I saw mercenaries flee.

And then – *BANG!*

One of the shots must have hit the crate, because the plasma cannon exploded. The blast was incredible. A tidal wave of energy swept across the slope, knocking mercenaries over like skittles, smashing down the tents and sending me and Marjorie flying off the snowmobile.

We tumbled over and looked up to see tents burning and stun guns going off on their own, firing wildly into the air. The blast had smashed oil drums and scattered their contents across the slope, so fires rose up everywhere. Lord Osthwait was on his knees, screaming at the goons to rescue the second cannon before the flames reached that one too.

"Come on!" I screamed.

I scrambled up and ran for the snowmobile, which had rolled onto its side. I tried to flip the machine back over, but my arms were too weak.

"Help me!" I cried.

Marjorie got alongside me and grabbed hold. Between us we had just enough strength left to yank the machine back onto its skis. We jumped on, and I turned us back towards the burning tents.

There was no other way to the cave – we still had to get past this camp. Smoke rose from the front of the snowmobile, and the engine spluttered as we sped towards the chaos.

"It's not going to make it!" Marjorie screamed.

"It has to!"

"Jake, that other cannon..."

I'd seen it. The second crate had caught fire. Even forty mercenaries weren't able to control the flames. We had to get through this camp before that cannon exploded.

A few of the mercenaries fired as we approached, but most were too busy trying to fight the flames or drag the burning crate clear of other fires. We shot through a wall of flames from an oil slick, and past another burning tent, screaming the whole way. The slope grew steeper; the snowmobile shuddered. Dark smoke gushed from the engine.

We passed another tent. Lord Osthwait, still on his knees, picked up a stun gun. Marjorie snatched it from his hands as we sped past.

"Jake, go faster!" she screamed.

I snatched a look back and saw mercenaries fleeing from the burning crate. We were only fifty metres away – was that far enough?

"Jake!" Marjorie shrieked.

The second cannon exploded.

I don't know if it was a more powerful weapon, or

that we were closer, but the blast wave picked us up and hurled us from the snowmobile. It was as if we'd been hit by a tornado; we flew though the air, whirling our arms and screaming. I crash-landed and looked up just in time to see the snowmobile coming at us, flipping over from the force of the explosion. I grabbed Marjorie and dragged her out of the way just as it tumbled past.

She was in a bad state. Her shoulder sagged as if it was dislocated, there was a deep cut across her cheek, and one of her legs had twisted at a nasty angle. She looked confused more than hurt, as if she had just woken from a nice sleep into the middle of all of this.

"You ... you saved my life," she rasped.

"Don't get used to it," I told her.

"Manchester United!"

From out of nowhere Tenzin rushed over to us, his robes snapping in the wind. He looked horrified, his eyes flicking from one scene of chaos to the next at the base of this sacred mountain.

He tried to help me stand, but my legs were too shaky. At first all I could do was lean against him, trying to stop my head from spinning, and assess the damage in my body. I felt like an elephant had used me as a trampoline; everything ached. But I couldn't collapse here. Down the slope, the mercenaries had begun to regroup.

The second explosion had scattered more oil across the slope and set fire to one of the helicopters, so fires now spread all the way across the hill. Lord Osthwait roared at his goons to go after me as he stamped out flames on his fur coat.

"Manchester United, what is happening?"

"Tenzin, we have to get to that cave."

His face changed again – from horror to something like sadness. He knew I still planned to find the Hall of Records. He could have stopped me by leaving me there – I don't think I could have made it to the cave alone – but still he helped. After a few steps, I stopped and looked back. Marjorie lay semi-conscious on the ground as the snow around her turned crimson. I had no idea what Lord Osthwait would do with her...

I cursed. "Tenzin, we have to take her too."

Tenzin didn't argue – helping an enemy came more naturally to him than to me. We staggered back and lifted her between us. I grabbed the stun gun she'd swiped and used it as a crutch to support me on one side as I carried Marjorie with the other. She was small and slim, but she felt like she weighed a ton.

"This way, Tenzin," I grunted. "That cave..."

The cave entrance was barely a metre wide, a crack in the rock that howled with the wind lashing through it, as if to warn us not to enter. We kept moving, pulling Marjorie with us. Her feet slid over the snow and through the crack and into the Crystal Mountain.

43

Well, this was tricky, the three of us in that cave: Tenzin glaring at me like he was considering giving up his monk's vows to strangle me; Marjorie – my sworn enemy – dazed and bleeding in my arms; and forty mercenaries outside, all set on revenge against me for blowing up their camp. I still had the stun gun we'd stolen from Lord Osthwait, which was the only reason they hadn't already charged into the cave. Instead we were under siege.

"So ... what now?" Marjorie wheezed.

Wind screeched through the cave opening, whipping in snow. Ice creaked and moaned, as if we'd entered the belly of some giant beast. Though the entrance was barely a metre across, it widened into a tunnel that seemed to be carved from ice. Only a few grey rocks sticking through the gleaming surface hinted at the cave walls beneath. The Drak Terma had suggested this cave led into the mountain, but the tunnel was only ten metres deep. I rushed to the rear wall and banged my fist against its frozen surface, feeling the thickness of the ice.

"If there's a way to the Hall of Records," I guessed, "it's hidden under this ice."

"The stun gun," Marjorie gasped, "should blast through it."

"Good thinking," I replied.

I fiddled with the weapon, trying to work out how it fired. My hands trembled so much I could barely hold it.

Tenzin had moved away and now sat at the side of the cave. His knees were drawn close to his chest; his head hung low. He'd saved me – *again* – and here I was – *again* – about to fire a weapon at the most sacred site in his religion. If I pulled the trigger it would break his heart. But if I didn't I would be caught, with no way left to save my family.

The stun gun trembled in my grip.

I thought of the promise I made to Takara and the monks of Yerpa Gompa. My family had wanted to keep that promise, even if it meant failing in our own mission. I knew they would *still* want to. I remembered my mum, and her devastated gaze around the wreckage of the First Emperor's tomb – the destruction I had caused. I remembered the lama's words, calm and heartfelt, before I set off to find the Drak Terma: *"To you Kailas is a place on a map. To us it is a place in the heart."*

It hadn't meant much at the time, but I was beginning to understand. All the things I had destroyed or seen ruined had meant little to me. This mountain didn't mean much to me either; it was just a mountain. But I had seen what it meant to others. I *felt* that. I wished I hadn't, because I really wanted to blast a hole in that ice wall.

I turned to Tenzin and his eyes were briefly hopeful, as if I might not fire the weapon after all. But my grip tightened on the stun gun as I thought of my family, and Tenzin bowed his head in despair.

44

Standing was a struggle. One of her legs had twisted in the fall from the snowmobile, and something had snapped in her knee. She sensed that she would probably never walk on that leg again, but it didn't matter. Most of the pain was numbed by the cold, and by the thrill that gave her the strength to rise: the thrill of a mission about to be accomplished.

She rose and reached into her pocket. The phurba was still there. Of course it was. They had come so far together. It wouldn't let her down now.

Jake had his back to her as he prepared to fire the stun gun at the back of the cave. She hobbled closer, gripped the knife even tighter.

Wind howled into the cave.

He had this coming. He always had to win, always had to fight. He never gave up, no matter what the cost. He had taken everything from her, and he didn't care at all. He didn't care about anything. Even now he was about to blast his way into a sacred mountain. He deserved this.

She slid the blade from her pocket.

Jake turned.

The stun gun trembled in his grip as he stared at her, and then at the boy monk who had helped them reach this cave.

The gun clattered to the cave floor.

His voice came out soft, but also like steel, a strength that caused Marjorie to limp back a step. She had listened to Jake for hundreds of hours on recordings from bugs planted in his house. She had heard him shout at his parents and scream at his sister, but she had never heard such strength or certainty in the four words he now whispered.

"I can't do it."

She stopped, her hand and the blade frozen.

"What?" she asked.

"I *won't* do it," Jake said.

He looked again to the boy monk, whose head rose from between his knees. A toothy smile rose across the boy's face, and Marjorie realized that they were friends.

"Manchester United?" the monk whispered.

"I broke my promise to you, Tenzin. But I'm making it again, and I'm sticking to it. This is as far as I go."

Majorie stared, struggling to understand. This

wasn't possible. He wasn't about to surrender to avoid damaging a mountain. He had *collapsed* a mountain in Honduras!

She felt a chill that had nothing to do with the wind or the snow.

"I don't understand," she said. "Your family..."

"They wouldn't want me to," he replied. "I can find another way to help them."

No! No, he couldn't do this! This was Jake Atlas, the destroyer – of treasures, tombs, lives and plans. He was a villain.

"I can't do it," Jake repeated.

A tune began to play in Marjorie's head. She heard it even above the wind and the storm, and the cries of the mercenaries outside the cave. *La Bohème.*

All the things she had lost. None of that was this boy's fault. He was just *a boy*. Why had she even come here?

Her arm slumped, and the phurba fell to the rocks.

"Neither can I," she whispered.

45

OK, I got it.

I understood the moment I saw the knife shaking in Marjorie's hand. She had planned to kill me. I wasn't angry, or surprised. In fact, I felt sorry for her as she slumped to her knees in the middle of the cave, and the last of her strength came out in a long, frost-cloud sigh.

I had always known there was a connection between us, a mad rivalry. My sister had said I was obsessed with her, and I'd denied it, while knowing she was right. But I realized then, as I stood over Marjorie in that frozen cave, that I didn't even know her. I knew her name, but almost nothing else other than this one fact: I had reduced her to this. She had an obsession too – she had been in charge of an operation. That was taken from her because of me, and she had wanted revenge.

But now she had given up on that too. All she had left was this cave and this storm and her broken dreams, and a tune she began to hum as she slumped to the ground and curled up, shivering.

I pulled off my coat and laid it over her as a blanket. I wouldn't last long without it in this cold, but I didn't need to, anyway – the mercenaries would storm this cave soon and I'd be caught.

Tenzin had stayed silent, watching this strange moment. I hadn't told him about her, and it didn't seem right to now. It didn't feel like a victory, and not just because we were still under siege. Too many people had lost for anyone to say they had won. Tenzin had lost his home, Marjorie had lost everything, and I had lost this hunt. But I had found something, too, along the way.

Tenzin leaned closer and nudged me with his shoulder.

"*Now* you see, Manchester United. No need for your smarty-goggles."

He never explained that comment, but he didn't need to. He had told me we saw things differently, and in many ways we still did. But I was beginning to change.

"Never gonna like yak butter tea," I replied.

Tenzin grinned, and I think we might have hugged, but Lord Osthwait bellowed at us from outside the cave. He'd found a megaphone and sounded more pompous than ever.

"Jake Atlas!" he boomed. "Marjorie Smith! There is no escape."

Marjorie *Smith*? I wouldn't have thought that. Tenzin and I tried to help her stand, but she just slumped into our arms. In the end, we sat her upright against the frozen wall. If part of her still wanted to see me get hurt, she had a great view.

"Jake Atlas!" roared the annoying aristocrat. "Your time is up!"

"You keep saying that!" I yelled. "But I'm still here and you're still there."

I was trying to sound cool, but my hands were shaking as I picked up the stun gun from the ground. Any moment now, they would storm this cave.

"Tenzin," I said. "If these guys realize we know each other, you'll become their enemy too. So don't say my name. Just act scared and they should leave you alone."

"But, Manchester United, you are my friend. I will not say I do not know you."

"You have to, Tenzin."

"I will not."

More shouts from outside. Lights from smart-goggles beamed through the cave entrance as the mercenaries stalked closer.

I aimed the stun gun at the sliver of night. I doubted I'd be able to put up much of a fight, but after everything I'd been through I wasn't walking out of here. They were going to have to drag me out.

"Just so you know, Tenzin, I'm going to fight."

"Do you have to?" he asked.

"Not really, but I don't want to surrender, not to these guys."

One of the mercenaries charged through the cave entrance. Light from smart-goggles dazzled my eyes, so it took me a second to react. I pulled the trigger on the stun gun, but nothing happened. I tried again, knowing already that the weapon must have broken in the explosion. The mercenary roared as he sprang at me in full attack.

If he'd got his hands on me he'd have dragged me from that cave in bloody pieces. But he didn't even touch me, because right then there was a flash of crimson, a flap of robe. A foot shot past me and connected with the mercenary's face, shattering his smart-goggles and breaking his nose with a sickening snap. A hand grabbed the guy's shoulder and he flipped over. His legs flew up and his head struck the cave floor. He lay on the rocks, groaning and dazed. Tenzin stood over him in the coolest fighting pose ever. My friend's jaw was set, his eyes sharp and narrow, and there was no trace of his usual smile. He had just taken this mercenary out with the coolest ninja moves I'd ever seen!

At first I couldn't think of anything to say.

"I... I thought you didn't fight?" I asked, finally.

Tenzin's jaw unlocked to let a smile rise across his cheeks. "*Do not* does not mean *cannot*, Manchester

United. Shaolin Kung Fu. We are sworn to defend Kailas."

"I... Why didn't you help me earlier, then?"

"Fighting is last resort, Manchester United."

"So you waited for me to get blown up until you joined in?"

"Yes, exactly."

I could hardly believe it. This whole time Tenzin was an expert fighter? It was good news, because Lord Osthwait was roaring orders again outside the cave.

"Can you fight forty of these goons?" I asked.

"I do not think so. But only two can fit through this entrance. So we fight one each."

"But one each *twenty times*?"

"Get ready," Tenzin said.

Outside the cave, torches flashed and boots crunched over snow. Tenzin got into his fighting pose, ready for action. I ditched the broken stun gun and tried to copy him, but I'm not sure I looked half as cool or confident. My hands trembled. My heart thumped faster, and my vision blurred with nervous sweat even in the freezing cave. One of my arms was so badly swollen that I could barely move it.

"Here they come!" I warned.

But they didn't. No one came.

We waited, ready for the attack. But no one entered. I glanced at Tenzin, who shrugged but didn't break his fighting stance. The wind settled for a second, and in the quiet I heard a grunt and a thud. Someone cried out, and a black-gloved hand flopped through the entrance. One of the mercenaries had collapsed outside the cave. Something had taken the goon out. Something was taking them *all* out.

"Manchester United? What is going on?"

"I think it's the guardian," I hissed. "It's the guardian of the mountain."

I felt cemented to the spot, a statue. It wasn't just fear that stopped me moving. Forty mercenaries scared me, but the creature that had followed me across Tibet, that had taken out Kyle and Veronika Flutes, and that was now outside this cave – that was pure terror.

"Have no fear," Tenzin whispered. "The guardian only hunts those who seek to enter this mountain. You are no longer its enemy, Manchester United."

Wasn't I? Was I sure? I did want to honour my promise to Tenzin, but part of me still wanted to reach the end of this hunt, to find out where the emerald tablets led...

"What if I'm not one hundred percent on that?" I asked.

"Then it will probably attack you, just in case."

"*What?*"

"Be calm. It is coming."

46

Outside the cave, the fighting had stopped. Wind screamed though the opening in the rock, and then silence, other than the rasping of my frantic breaths. The black-gloved hand that had fallen through the entrance slid back as something dragged the mercenary's body away from the cave. It was clearing a path to reach us.

"Get back!" I wailed. "Get back or I'll—"

"Jake?" a voice called. "Jake, is that you?"

"*Mum?*"

I heard my dad call out too, and then my sister, and a second later they all rushed into the cave. There was no guardian monster out there – it was them!

I fell to my knees. My body turned from concrete to wet paper, and I dropped, totally spent. Mum rushed to catch me and wrapped me in a hug. Dad hugged me next, and I think Pan did as well, but

I was too dazed to be sure. Of course I was delighted to see them, but also relieved that a monster hadn't stormed into the cave, and that Tenzin and I were no longer alone.

They had come for me.

About time, too.

I could see from the storm of bruises down Mum's face, Dad's black eye beneath his broken glasses and the cut across Pan's nose that their journey here had been just as tough as ours. Seeing my family like that reminded me how much I'd missed them. It hurt to think they had been in danger and I wasn't there.

Not that they *needed* my help. I found out later that they had guessed I'd been caught, and made the same decision to reach Kailas, to save me. But I didn't understand how they had found me in this cave without the Drak Terma.

"How did you know I was here?" I asked.

Mum smiled and wiped dirt off my cheek. "We just followed the chaos."

Pan looked baffled by all of this. She swept the torch on her smart-goggles around the ice walls, and then at Marjorie, who smiled weakly at us from the side of the cave.

"Why is *she* here?" Pan asked. She shifted her glare to Tenzin. "Or him?"

"Tenzin helped me get here," I rasped. "He saved my life. About ten times, I think."

Mum couldn't help herself – she grabbed Tenzin

and hugged him too. "Thank you," she whispered.

"Welcome," Tenzin said.

Dad already had his serious face on as he paced the sides of the cave, examining the thick ice that covered the walls. "So this cave leads into the mountain?" he asked.

"According to the Drak Terma," I replied. "Maybe there's a door behind the ice. But this is as far as we can go."

Dad nudged his glasses back up his nose and looked at me through their shattered lenses. "What?"

"We can't enter this mountain," I insisted. "It's sacred."

He stared at me for a long moment, and then looked at Mum. They had another of their silent exchanges, only this time it ended with them smiling.

"So you weren't here to find the Hall of Records?" Mum asked. "You were here to defend the mountain."

"I guess so," I muttered.

"Manchester United was brave," Tenzin said.

Pan looked at Tenzin as if I'd told her he was our bitter enemy. "So, what, you have a new partner now?" she asked me. "He's not your twin, you know."

"I know, Pan."

She shrugged and redirected her torchlight at the rear wall of the cave. "So, let me get this straight. All this time we've been after the Hall of Records, and now all that's in our way is a little bit of ice, but we're not even going to look?"

"That's right," I said.

Pan shrugged. "Cool."

"So, what now?" I asked.

Mum stopped smiling. Her face went all serious – narrow eyes and tight jaw – and she touched
the amulet around her neck, a sure sign of impend-
ing trouble.

"There's something you should see," she told me.

Tenzin and I followed them out of the cave and
into the night. The wind had calmed, and fires flared
around the slope where slicks of oil still burned from
the explosion. Zigzag lines of flame cast orange flick-
ers across the snow. Around them, mercenaries lay
unconscious where they had been taken out by my
family.

Only Lord Osthwait had escaped. He was charging downhill, slipping over and staggering up,
waving his arms and calling for help.

Further down the slope, near the lake, other lights
moved. At first it seemed like a wall of light coming
towards us – but they were *different* lights, moving
together. Some were headlights of snowmobiles
or ski tanks, others super-lumen beams of smart-
goggles. Engines roared, crawler tracks churned up
snow, and gruff voices barked commands as the silhouette army marched towards us up the slope.

"They're not just mercenaries, are they?" I asked.

"They're hunters," Dad said. "About fifty of them.
We met a few on the way here, but news spread and

now they all know where we are."

"They all want that billion dollars?"

"No," Pan replied. "They all suspect something big is hidden in this mountain. Most are coming for that. We're just a bonus."

I turned and looked up at Mount Kailas, a black giant that seemed to sway gently as puffy grey clouds drifted past its sheer cliffs.

"We can't let them," I said. "I promised Tenzin I'd protect this mountain."

"I know," Mum agreed. "We'll do our best."

"I'll help," Tenzin added.

"Tenzin's a ninja," I explained.

Dad glanced at him, but didn't look too surprised. "We ran into Kyle and Veronika Flutes on the way here," he said. "They were unconscious. Was that you?"

How could I answer that? Just the memory of what I'd heard outside Chui Gompa was more terrifying than this whole hoard of hunters. None of my family would believe me, and, anyway, I didn't even know what *had* taken Kyle and Veronika out. I hadn't seen anything, after all.

"No," I said. "That was something else."

"Another hunter?"

"No. Just ... something else."

I shielded my face as a searchlight beamed from one of the hunter's vehicles, picking me out in front of the cave. Other lights shone on Tenzin and my⁻

family as the hunters stalked closer, black against the glare of their own lights. They looked like a proper nasty bunch.

"There's still time to flee if we want to," Dad suggested.

He sounded hopeful, and I didn't blame him – running would be the easier and less painful option. But these hunters weren't coming for us. They were coming for the mountain I'd promised to protect.

"Remember," Mum said, "this doesn't have to be a fair fight. Use whatever you can to take them down. They'll underestimate you because you're young. Use that against them. Go for them wherever it hurts."

I glanced at Pan and then Tenzin, and we all grinned. It was funny, we had been on this hunt for what seemed like for ever. I had been so obsessed with winning, but right now we were about to lose and it somehow felt right. We were about to fail for something we believed in. We were making a stand.

"May I join you?" a voice croaked.

Marjorie crawled alongside us. She looked shattered, her trembling hand barely able to hold her own knife. She wouldn't be much help, but I nodded.

"Good to have you with us," I said.

Weirdly, she started to cry. That lady had a lot of issues, but I didn't have time to worry about them.

Now the hunters were coming.

We should have been focused on the danger ahead, but Tenzin turned and stared at the rock ledge above the cave. "Manchester United? I think someone else is coming to join us."

That did not sound good.

"Oh, God…" I whispered.

"What is it, Jake?" Mum demanded.

"Remember the lama warned us about the guardian spirit of this mountain? That's what took out Kyle and Veronika."

"It is OK," Tenzin assured us. "The guardian is on our side. We are all protecting the mountain, so we are safe." He was grinning now, wider than I had ever seen him – and I'd seen him grin a *lot*. "Now these hunters are the ones in trouble."

I turned back to face the hunters. I could see their faces, slavering like wild dogs closing in on a kill. I guessed they had agreed to catch us first and then combine forces to find the secret in the mountain.

I remembered something the lama said at Yerpa Gompa: *"In this land legends are not always just legends."*

Above me I heard bare feet on rock, the thumping feet of something far heavier than a human. There was a grunt and a snort, and then the same sound I heard as I hid at Chui Gompa – that savage, spitting roar. It came from above, and I saw its shadow before I saw what caused it, before it leaped from the ledge and over our heads – before the guardian of the mountain landed in front of us in the snow.

And what did we see?

I can't tell you. I mean, I saw it well enough for the memory to haunt me. I still see it every time I close my eyes, like someone tattooed its image on the back of my eyelids. But I promised I wouldn't tell. The guardian of the mountain is sacred to the monks of Yerpa Gompa. It lives in secrecy among secluded ranges, far from human eyes, and only emerges from hiding when it senses danger to the Crystal Mountain.

You may not believe that. I'm not sure I would had I not seen it with my own eyes. But the more people know about it, the more they will seek it out. A value will be placed on it. Hunters will come. Eventually someone will find it, and someone will catch it.

I made a promise to the monks that I would keep the guardian's secret, and I intend to honour that too. Just take my word for it – you do not want to seek it, or catch it, or get anywhere near it.

It's big.

And hairy.

That's all I'll say.

To be honest, I was so terrified that I barely saw much more. My family staggered back, Tenzin and Marjorie too, each trying to protect one another in case the guardian turned against us. But Tenzin was right; the creature seemed to know that we weren't its enemy. It was only interested in the hunters.

Even together they didn't stand a chance against this beast rampaging across the slope. It threw them in the air, smashed them across the snow, destroyed

307

their machines and caused their dogs to cower, whimpering, behind rocks. These hunters had travelled the world, seen crazy things, but none of them had ever witnessed anything so savage. Most of them just fled. A few got past the guardian, but we mopped them up easily enough.

Mum and Dad did what they were best at, and Tenzin was all flips and flying kicks, which were so incredible that at times I just stopped to watch. Pan and I joined in as best we could, jumping on backs and gouging eyes, and even Marjorie found the strength to hurl a few rocks, although they didn't achieve much. She looked happy, though. Once the terror of seeing the guardian had passed, and we knew it was on our side, we *all* looked happy. At one point, around the time the last few hunters fled, taking a pleading Lord Osthwait with them in their jeep, I looked back at the mountain we had come so far to find, the Crystal Mountain, and finally I understood that name. A crystal is something pure and clean, something perfect. Something worth fighting for.

Moonlight shimmered against its sheer western face, reflecting off ice fields and rock ledges, entrances to caves that hid secrets we would never uncover. The silvery light came together in a curving slash, a crescent.

The mountain was smiling.

47

"You have been on quite a journey."

The lama topped up my yak butter tea, and then hung the pot over the fire he'd lit on the mountainside. He breathed in the steam, which for a second seemed to smooth all the wrinkles on his face. He looked at me and smiled. I hadn't thought anyone could out-smile Tenzin, but this guy had him beat. I wondered if he'd been chosen to lead the monastery just because he had the biggest grin. It seemed as good a reason as any.

"Did you find your treasure?" he asked.

I sipped the tea, grateful for its warmth. I'd spent so long in the cold that parts of me still seemed to be thawing.

"Not this time," I replied.

The lama's glasses glinted as he watched a Himalayan vulture swoop circles over the valley.

"Ah," he said, "but perhaps this time you really did."

These monks loved speaking in riddles, but I was beginning to understand.

We stood together watching monks clear rocks from the avalanche that had destroyed their home. It would take them months to rebuild Yerpa Gompa. Once I had healed I'd stay as long as I could to help; not just to keep my promise, but because I wanted to.

My family had helped Tenzin recreate his chorten from its rubble, and he'd prayed to his monastery's founder for permission to rebuild his home. But the moment he was reunited with his fellow monks, I think he realized that he had never really needed that permission. He *was* home.

He came with us back across Tibet in a jeep that one of the hunters had abandoned. We told our stories, sang songs, stared at a billion stars. Tenzin taught us the yak dance too, as we camped. We kept an eye out for hunters and mercenaries, but we were pretty sure they were occupied with their own problems, for a while, at least. Most had fled without provisions, and we'd sabotaged every other vehicle they left behind. They were tough people, so they would survive, but they'd have a hard time getting across this land. Maybe their journeys would be good for them, like mine had been.

Marjorie came with us too. She sat in the back of the jeep and didn't say anything for the whole trip. She kept humming the same tune, with this strange smile

– not her usual arrogant smirk, but an actual smile. The humming got pretty annoying, but Mum insisted we let her be. She wasn't our friend, she was... Well, I don't know what she was now. Not our enemy.

My family were staying here too; we were camping with the monks down in the valley. Mum had taken over the building project. She kept muttering about "health and safety issues", but she totally loved bossing everyone around. She'd not touched her amulet once since we left the mountain. I wondered if she still thought about what happened here all those years ago with Takara. Defending Kailas and helping these monks – was she still trying to make up for that tragedy?

Pan, too, seemed happier. She'd made friends with Tenzin and they spent a lot of time talking about complicated religious things. I was a bit jealous at first – Tenzin was *my* friend! – but after a while it made me smile to see them together. I knew that even after we left, we would see Tenzin again. This place, its legends, its people – it was a part of us now. We'd be back one day. If nothing else I wanted Tenzin to teach me some of his ninja skills.

Only Dad seemed on edge. It was weird, because he'd always been the most relaxed of us all. He'd apologized a dozen times for leaving me to cross Tibet alone. I assured him it was fine, but that didn't seem to settle his mind. Since we'd arrived at the monk's valley he'd kept watch almost constantly. I didn't know why, and it would take me a long time to find out, but it was obvious that this adventure hadn't been a good thing for him. Eventually, it would lead to a disaster – but that's another story.

So what now?

Well, we still had a mission. The People of the Snake, and what they were trying to hide – none of that had been solved. We'd not found the answers we were looking for in Tibet, but I was sure the lost civilization would have left other markers. Only, getting this far had almost broken us. Even after we had healed, could we start over? Where, even, would we start?

All those thoughts whirled in my head as I stood with the lama on that mountainside, sipping yak butter tea. I felt fixed, I felt broken. I was hopeful, and I was full of doubt. And still, actually, full of questions. Some things that had happened on the mission still didn't quite make sense.

"What is it you wish to ask?" the lama said.

Seriously, this guy should have a stage show – as well as his riddles, he seemed to be a mind reader. But since he'd asked...

Something had nagged at me since that cave in the mountain. If Tenzin was such a great fighter, why hadn't he tried to stop me firing the gun at the mountain? He couldn't have known the weapon was broken. The more I thought about it, only one answer made sense.

"That cave," I asked. "Did it really lead to the Hall of Records?"

The lama cleaned his glasses on his robe, blinking in the fierce Tibetan sun. "I doubt it," he said.

"But ... the Drak Terma led me there."

"Did it?"

Across the avalanche site, Tenzin stopped working and flashed me one of his trademark grins. Did he know what the lama was talking about? Pan noticed too.

The lama didn't need to say any more; I understood. After his chorten was destroyed, Tenzin told me he'd known I had the Drak Terma. What I hadn't realized was that he'd told the pilgrims we met. He'd warned them I might ask for a translation. Those words they wrote for me were just gibberish.

Pan looked baffled, but I was grinning now at Tenzin. That entire time he'd been in total control.

"That cave," I said. "It was just a cave."

"Well, it was probably sacred," the lama replied. He slid his glasses back on and winked at me. "*Everything's* sacred to us."

I smiled, but I had another question. "When I came here first," I asked, "you refused to let us see the Drak Terma. Was that a test?"

"It was."

"So I guess I failed pretty spectacularly," I muttered.

"Perhaps," the lama replied. "Or perhaps not." He nodded to one of the monks, who had been waiting for this moment. The monk carried over a small wooden box, about the size of a Rubik's Cube, and held it out for me to take.

I hesitated, looking to Mum, Dad, Pan and then Tenzin, who had all stopped working to see what was going on. Each of them smiled, signalling for me to accept whatever this was. The monk held it closer, so I put my tea down on a rock and took the gift.

I almost dropped it in shock as I saw it properly. It was decorated on every side with the same strange script we'd seen on the emerald tablets. Carved on each side, too, was the mysterious symbol of the lost civilization – the snake eating its own tail.

The box had no obvious lid, although I felt something inside slide and knock against the wood. Whatever it was, it was incredibly light...

"In there you will find everything you seek," the lama said. "All the lost knowledge once hidden in the Crystal Mountain. It is yours to use as you see fit, with our blessing."

Whoa!

It was such a shock that I almost dropped it. I gripped it tighter, with hands that began to shake. Mum gasped; my sister laughed.

"I ... *All* of it?" I asked. "The whole Hall of Records is in this box?"

I was expecting a riddle about how big things come in small packages, but the lama just smiled.

"This knowledge is not what makes Kailas sacred,"

he explained, "but as long as it remains there, the mountain will be a target. Our only request is that you let it be known that you have this information, to any that might seek it."

I got it; he wanted to make sure no one else turned up at Kailas with plasma cannons. None would if there was nothing left to find. I knew my family would agree, and so I nodded, still staring at the box and its intricately carved lid.

"Are you going to open it?" the lama asked.

The box trembled in my hands. Everyone was watching, waiting. Even the monks scurried closer, eager to see what was inside. But I didn't open the box. I set it down on the rocks beside my tea.

"Not yet," I replied. "There's work to do here first."

I expected one of my family to protest, but none of them said a word. Dad ruffled my hair in a way he hadn't done in ages, and Pan shrugged, and Mum smiled, and we all got busy working again, helping the monks to rebuild their home. Whatever was in that box, I was certain it would lead to new adventures, fresh discoveries, lost tombs or temples. Maybe, even, it would save millions of lives. But all of that could wait, just for a short time. I had a promise to keep, and a friend to help. Perhaps, I realized, as I gazed at the scene around me on that mountainside, not all treasure is found in tombs.

ABOUT THE AUTHOR

Rob Lloyd Jones never wanted to be a writer when
he grew up – he wanted to be Indiana Jones. So he
studied Egyptology and archaeology and went on
trips to faraway places. But all he found were interesting stories, so he decided to write them down.
Jake Atlas and the Quest for the Crystal Mountain
is Rob's fifth novel, although he has written over
ninety other books for children, including non-
fiction and adaptations of such classics as *Beowulf*.

About writing *Jake Atlas*, he says, "It began
on a rainy day in the countryside. Stuck at home,
I watched an Indiana Jones movie and then a
Mission: Impossible film straight after. I wondered
if you could mix the two: classic treasure hunts but
with crazy high-tech gadgets. I especially wanted
to set the first adventure in Egypt, a place and
history that I'd loved so much since studying it at

university. But I didn't really have a story, just an idea. Then, after becoming a father, I realized that many parents are invisible in stories for young people. I decided to write about a whole family on an adventure together. But not just any family – one with troubles and squabbles, special skills and deep secrets..."

Rob lives in a crumbling cottage in Sussex, where he writes and runs and moans about mud.

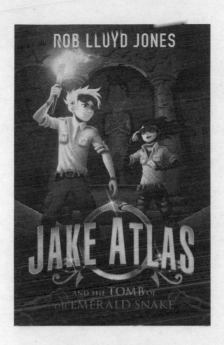

JAKE ATLAS
TOMB ROBBER,
TREASURE HUNTER,
TROUBLEMAKER

A couple of days ago I was a schoolboy
with terrible grades and even worse
behaviour – and a way of causing trouble
that drove people nuts.

Now I am a member of a super high-tech
treasure-hunting team searching for a lost
tomb so I can save my parents from being
turned into mummies by an evil cult.

Things have moved pretty fast...

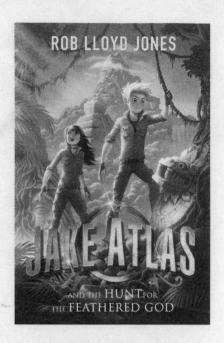

JAKE ATLAS
TOMB ROBBER,
TREASURE HUNTER,
TROUBLEMAKER

Jake Atlas and his family are on the run.
They're on a mission to stop the mysterious
People of the Snake from hiding the
secret to the history of humankind.

But the international police are
chasing Jake and his family through
the jungles of Honduras – one of the
most dangerous places in the world.

The second thrilling Jake Atlas adventure.